Roddy Murray

A Snow White Scenario

Acknowledgements

A big thank you to Sandy Murray and Margaret Rustad for their help and assistance with the text and storyline. A thank you to Dr Mairi Burton for her advice on medical matters.

As ever a huge thank you to Pauline MacGillivray and our ever growing family without whom this book would have been finished six months ago.

By the same author;

Body and Soul

The Treasure Hunters

George Milne – Cat Detective

George Milne - Murder at the Butler's Convention

For my parents and for my children.

Chapter 1 - Another Convenient Accident

Nigel looked out of his window at the rain bouncing off the street outside.

"Shit," he cursed knowing he had finished all the drink in the house the night before and would have to walk the quarter of a mile to the local convenience store. He always reckoned it was misnamed: there was nothing convenient about walking a quarter of a mile in the rain.

He hated going outside at all, never mind in the rain, but he hated being sober even more. He grabbed a pair of filthy trousers and a torn raincoat and shoved on his shoes without tying the laces. They leaked and he knew his feet would be wet and cold when he returned. That didn't matter; it was more important to get more vodka and re-enter oblivion. He pulled the door shut and locked it. It was the one thing he did meticulously every time he entered or exited his flat. He was scared somebody would enter it and ransack it again. He knew they could get in, whether he locked it or not, but the delay might just be enough to slow them down. Either way he wanted to know if somebody was waiting for him when he returned.

It had happened before when they had tried to scare him off and it had worked. That was until recently, when he had been approached by the news agency and eventually agreed to provide a statement on the abuse he had suffered as a child. Partly he still wanted revenge but he was realistic enough to know that was unlikely to happen. Mainly he was tired of it all. Tired of life and decided to spill the beans and to hell with the consequences. The reporter he dealt with assured him he would be safer if his story was in the public domain, and Nigel had tried to convince himself that he was telling all in part to protect himself. A deeper part of him knew that he was inviting death to come sooner.

He shuffled down the pavement on his side of the street and headed for the shop. The rain was heavy and he kept his head down and scrunched up in the worn hood of the coat. His feet had got soaked straight away when his shoes touched the pavement. He didn't care. He only cared about getting to the shop, buying three bottles of vodka and getting home again. He only cared about that so that he could get drunk again and stop caring about anything at all.

He paid no attention to the rain, his wet feet or the large black four wheel drive vehicle that slowly pulled out of its parking space when he left the flat and followed behind him at a safe distance. He paid so little attention to anything that the vehicle was able to time its acceleration perfectly to hit him at the corner of his street before he could look up and see it coming.

If he tried to jump out the way it wasn't obvious to the driver, who aimed at Nigel square on and hit him at forty miles an hour. Nigel never stood a chance and maybe didn't want to. The driver stopped just long enough to look back. Through the patch of the rear window cleared by the windscreen wiper he saw Nigel lie still with his neck clearly broken, and drove off with a look of satisfaction on his face. Job done!

Chapter 2 - Birthday Girl

Susan White was sitting in Brian Smithe's office in Portcullis House on her birthday looking at the five cards which had arrived that day. Five was more than some would get, she knew, but it wasn't many. On this particular day she had got her hopes up when a total of ten cards were delivered by internal mail. Unfortunately five had been for a newly elected MP in the Opposition. Somehow it seemed worse that the woman concerned who shared a birthday was part of Her Majesty's Opposition. Not only was she against everything Sue was helping Brian work for, but she had now stolen five birthday cards too. She put the cards back into internal mail, hoping that they would arrive at least a day late. The insult was compounded later in the day when a massive bouquet of flowers was also erroneously delivered to her. She made a point of keeping the flowers as compensation for the cards.

Just as she finished arranging the flowers in a vase, Sir Crispin Jessop, The Chief Whip, entered Brian's office without knocking. Sue immediately felt a pang of fear, as she always did whenever she saw him. She suspected everybody felt the same. The whips were an evil lot, from what she could see, but Sir Crispin had an air about him beyond that of the others. Brian always said you could smell a hint of sulphur after Jessop left, as if you had narrowly escaped the attention of the devil himself.

"Where's Smithe?" he asked, ignoring the flowers and the cards which indicated it was Sue's birthday.

"I'm not sure," she stammered, relieved he wasn't here to investigate a missing bouquet. "I think he is having lunch with his wife."

Sir Crispin stared at her briefly, as if assessing the truth of her answer, then left. Sue had just breathed a sigh of relief when Jessop's head re-appeared round the door.

"Tell him I want to see him asap if you happen to see him before I do."

He looked at the flowers in an odd way and Sue nearly wet herself with fear.

"Oh, and Happy Birthday!" he added without emotion before leaving for good. She felt like a mouse who had been complimented on her whiskers by a cat passing by on its way to catch fatter prey.

As a researcher she found herself sitting in the midst of Brian's office on a regular basis with very little to do. At times he needed information for a speech or committee appearance but a lot of the time that came from elsewhere. Often Brian would come into the office and just sit and talk. She didn't mind really but it wasn't what she had expected. Offered the post after graduation, largely on the back of her dissertation regarding state benefits and the correlation to birth rates which Brian had plagiarised wildly for a number of speeches and op-ed pieces in the press, she had at first been flattered. It was only later she realised that she had been brought into his team for two reasons: firstly to stop her complaining about his use of her work, and secondly because he fancied her.

The latter reason became clear after a late sitting when the government had won a narrow vote on cutting benefits. Brian had asked her to work on, ostensibly to research any points raised by the opposition so that they could be countered during the debate. A number of blows were struck and she came up with counter points to each, but when Brian popped in during a recess he seemed more concerned with whether she had eaten or not than any information she had come up with. After the vote he had again raised the question of food and suggested they ate in a restaurant he knew which served food most of the night. Again she had been flattered and had drunk a little bit more than she should have. One thing led to another, as the saying goes, and they had ended up back at a piedà-terre which Brian rented at tax-payers' expense and, after drinking more wine, they had spent the night together.

The next day Brian had been very contrite about his behaviour but also very caring and understanding. They agreed that what had happened should remain a secret to them alone and went to work that day by separate routes. Their initial plan failed miserably and they spent many more nights together over the following few months. Sue believed that Brian had fallen in love with her, largely because he had told her so, and for her part, she felt something approaching love for him, or at least was in love with the thought of being an MP's wife and perhaps parliamentary candidate herself at some date in the future.

When she discovered that she was pregnant she was shocked. Brian was even more shocked, but they talked through the situation and he promised that he would extricate himself from his 'loveless marriage' as soon as he could and they would be together. She believed him and went on to have lovely, healthy twins. She kept away from Parliament and focused all her energies on the boys. At first Brian would phone and occasionally visit but both the calls and the visits tailed off to the extent that Sue became concerned. A nagging doubt formed in her head despite Brian's constant reassurances that he was working on a smooth process of leaving his wife and getting divorced, but as a Minister the timing never seemed to be right.

Eventually the landlady where Sue was living became suspicious of her cover story regarding the twins' father and Sue had to move out. Initially this was into a small hotel, then a bed and breakfast to save money. As time passed however, she had to move from there too and Brian assured her that he would arrange for his private secretary to find something suitable for the long term.

Chapter 3 - A highly convenient crisis.

As the days rolled by towards the General Election the Prime Minister and his team watched as the floating voters moved their support back and forward, but were dismayed to notice overall that the opposition was gaining and keeping more voters each time. More and more polls suggested that they might form the next government, and this was unacceptable in the PM's view. It was also unacceptable in the view of most of his cabinet and the many wealthy party donors who expected a decent return on their money and didn't fancy having to shell out to gain influence with the other side too.

A second term was in such danger that the party chairman, Sir Marcus Digby, had to call a crisis meeting to look at drastic action to correct the swing in the polls. After welcoming everyone to the Churchill dining room in Dudley's Club he set out the threat they were all facing.

"In most years, getting elected is simple. Young people don’t vote so ignore them. Old people vote in droves so scare them into fearing the opposition will steal their pensions and savings. Enough of the floating voters of working age need to believe that we can make them better off than any other party. That usually only takes a few months each time. Once we're in power we can largely do what we like for four and a half years. At the moment however, we are facing an electorate who are feeling the pinch financially and are blaming us. The press have been doing their best on our behalf to blame the Opposition but recently without success. We have been in power too long now to claim it's the mess we inherited; people now blame us for any mess and sadly the other side have started to look a bit too competent for my liking. In short we will not be re-elected if voters believe we are not going to make them better off."

"Surely people don't trust the Opposition with their savings or pensions as usual? We need to re-emphasise these dangers till the voters switch back to us," suggested one of the younger ministers present.

"They don't trust us either, going by the latest from our focus groups and what we have gleaned from our contacts in Labour's focus group machinery," answered Sir Marcus. "Voters seem to feel the money they are paying in taxes is lining the pockets of our supporters rather than providing better opportunities for them and their children. Austerity and lower public spending have gone out of fashion and we need something new."

"What else can we scare the voters with?" asked Sir Crispin Jessop, the party's Chief Whip.

There was a pause amongst the assembled senior party figures before the Chancellor added hopefully, "What about the War on Terror? It used to work."

"My dear boy," said Sir Marcus. "Not even American voters buy that one anymore, not after Iraq."

"It is the right approach though," said the Prime Minister, Charles Pearson. "If we have a credible threat to national security and to everyone's safety walking the streets we might be able to exploit the Opposition's weakness on defence. We need to catch some terrorists in the act or some such thing. Sir Gregory: any ideas?"

Sir Gregory Noble, Head of MI5, looked up from his notes somewhat surprised. He was not a party figure after all and was there to provide advice on security matters and also because he had been at school with Sir Marcus.

"Our role is to assess and advise on security threats rather than conjure them up for electoral purposes," he advised in a tone suggesting something of a reprimand. Prime Minister or not, he wasn't going to knuckle down to a boy who only started at his school during his own final year. Having made that point though he continued, "There are many security threats which we are monitoring at any moment in time, some more credible than others. It is not impossible that one of them could proceed further than was usual before being prevented. That would almost certainly gain more publicity and indeed recognition, than those we nip in the bud."

Sir Marcus nodded in agreement, suggesting to the others that a decision had been made.

"I'll leave the details to you and Marcus then," said the PM. "I have a meeting with the Queen shortly and need to get fully briefed for that. Unfortunately she tends to be pretty clued up on everything. Come on, Sir Geoffrey."

With that, the PM and his PPS, Sir Geoffrey Stanning, left, followed soon afterwards by the other figures, leaving only Sir Marcus and Sir Gregory at the table. A member of Dudley's staff closed the doors of the dining room behind the last of the other men and left them in peace to plan future events which might prove more conducive to a second term in office.

Chapter 4 - Free Accommodation

David Thomson signed on to his computer and started searching through the various pages he had just been given access to. None of them constituted national secrets as such, from what he could see, but it was an interesting collection of facts and figures regarding government resources and spending. After twenty minutes or so he found what he had been looking for: a list of government -owned or retained residences in the central London area. It was a large list which included everything from The Speaker's residence within the Palace of Westminster to a grace and favour home for a distant cousin of foreign royalty. Neither of those options helped him with his current task.

After two hours of searching properties and checking occupancy with the relevant department, he broke for coffee. After a further two hours he stopped for a late lunch. Just as he was about to give up hope he stumbled on a relatively new entry rented by the Home Office, some eighteen months previously. A couple of discreet enquiries confirmed that it was empty, and a further phone call using the Minister's clout led him to a key holder who could let him see it that evening.

He spent the intervening time catching up with his routine work of sorting correspondence and tweeting on behalf of the minister. When the time for the viewing arrived he grabbed his coat and took a taxi to the address of the empty property, making sure he kept a receipt in order to reclaim the cost.

He arrived at a substantial mews property in a quiet back lane which ran in front of a dozen or so similar properties. Each property had a double garage built-in which explained the huge cost to the tax payer in such a central area.

The property agent he had spoken to earlier was waiting at the front door with keys but had obviously already been inside the property to check it over.

"I was wondering when this one would be needed," he said, "Although I hadn't expected your department to need it. It is all arranged through the Home Office, though after almost two years it's never been used as far as I know."

"Share and share alike," said David vaguely as he followed the agent through the door.

The property was built over two floors. On the ground floor were a large lounge, a cloakroom, and a large dining kitchen with a connecting door to the double garage. Beyond the kitchen was a utility room with the usual white goods and a walk-in pantry. From the small window of the pantry, David could see the rear courtyard was small and had been concreted over. The walls had severe looking razor wire around them and the gate in the rear wall was a very solid looking steel affair.

The two men walked up the stairs to find it had two large bedrooms with four single beds crammed into each with an additional single bedroom and a bathroom with two separate shower cubicles instead of a bath and two wash-hand basins.

"It's never been used since the alterations were done," said the property agent.

"You mean the Home Office had it set up like this and then forgot about it?"

"I guess so."

After he had had the full tour David decided to make use of the empty property at least on a temporary basis.

"My department will be needing to use the property on a temporary basis, so if you could give me a set of keys that would be good, thanks."

“I can’t do that,” the agent replied. “Not without specific notification from the Home Office.”

“I believe you look after a number of properties in Central London for a range of Government departments. Part of the arrangement provides accommodation for you and your wife. I suggest you just give me a set of keys and the necessary authorisation will follow in due course. We are a bit pushed for time on this one.”

David held out his hand to receive the keys and stared at the property agent in as intimidating a manner as he could. After a pause while the man weighed up the pros and cons and having Googled David’s details before the meeting to make sure he was who he said he was, he eventually handed over a set of keys. He did, however, insist first that David signed a receipt for them.

After the agent had left, David immediately phoned Sue at the Bed and Breakfast and told her to get her things together within the hour as he had found more suitable and permanent accommodation for her. How permanent he couldn’t say but there was certainly plenty of room; even a bedroom each for the twins. He ignored her protests that she had only just managed to settle them down to sleep and said he would collect her in exactly an hour’s time. Again he reminded her not to speak to anyone except himself or Brian Smithe about her situation.

Chapter 5 - A New Home

As David helped Sue White into the mews house they probably looked for all the world like a young couple moving into their next home; a bigger home now that they had two babies to accommodate. Any onlookers might have been disappointed that he did not carry his bride across the threshold, and had they been closer they would have been surprised at the language he used as he struggled to prise the double buggy through the doorway.

Once inside David ran through the groceries he had bought and stored while she had been packing and advised he would supply essentials on a regular basis. Then, as the twins had mercifully remained asleep in their carrying chairs, he gave Sue a grand tour of the flat.

When she had seen the two bedrooms with eight beds crammed into them she giggled.

"Was this set up for Snow White and the seven dwarves?"

"Your guess is as good as mine, although they included a small bedroom for the huntsman or the wicked step-mother," replied David as he showed her the small single bedroom on the far side of the bathroom.

"Why two showers and no bath?" asked Sue. "I love a bath and there must have been room for both, although the two sinks could be handy for washing the twins simultaneously."

"Again I have no idea," said David in all honesty. "The previous tenants had it set up this way and then lost interest. Maybe the dwarves were frightened they'd drown in a bath."

After the confines of the Bed and Breakfast with its daily struggle to resist inquisitive questions from the couple who ran it, the house seemed like heaven to Sue. It even had a bedroom for each of the twins so that they wouldn't automatically set each other off whenever one woke up.

"I'll take it," she joked as if she had a choice.

David smiled politely at her comment and then advised her that he had to rush home.

Chapter 6 - The Minister for Unmarried Mothers

"How can we trust a single word the minister tells us when it changes from week to week?" asked the honourable member for Midsley West to cheers from his own benches and jeers from the Government side.

"The honourable member must rephrase that question," advised The Speaker when the noise level finally subsided in the chamber.

"Okay, I will. Last month you told us the number of single mothers on benefits, living in poverty with their children, was decreasing under this government but now, corrected by a national newspaper, you are admitting the number has in fact increased under this government by almost twenty percent. Is the Minister for Families creating more mothers living in poverty or not? Which is true?"

The Minister for Families looked flustered, well aware that he had been caught out providing dubious figures to parliament.

"I think the facts are quite clear and I stand by my statement today," he added in as confident a manner as he could muster.

"So half of what you tell this house is a pack of lies?" thundered the ageing figure from Midsley West.

"You will retract that," demanded The Speaker.

"Okay, only half of what you tell this house is true."

"No, I'm not having that," said The Speaker, whose patience had grown thin of late with several of the regular troublemakers. "You are suspended for use of un-parliamentary language. Yes ,you jolly well are suspended; again."

There were cheers from the Government's side and shouts of 'shame!' from Labour as Midsley's finest rose slowly to his feet, took his walking stick and did his best to stride out of the Commons with dignity.

The Minister for Families knew that this particular piece of pantomime was only delaying the inevitable. Now that he had been softened up by The Midsley Monster he would have to face a grilling from the Shadow Minister for Families, Dawn Harper. Harper the Harpie had missed her calling as a top QC and had instead dedicated her life to fighting the corner of the working classes. She hated Conservatives, the stuffiness of Parliament's gentleman's-club-feel, and hated male ministers in particular. She now scented blood and had tabled a number of questions regarding Brian Smithe's revision of the figures on unmarried mothers living in poverty, in private accommodation paid for with public funds.

"I would be obliged if the minister would confirm that the figures he has provided today, showing a twenty percent increase in single mothers living in poverty during the current government's time in office, are in fact correct."

Brian struggled through an answer to that and many other questions like it, trying not to sound as if he was completely incompetent, but aware that his opposite number was trying to convey that exact message. As he sat down for the final time he sneaked a look at Chief Whip who appeared to be writing something in a small, leather bound notebook.

"Shit," Brian thought. "That isn't good."

Chapter 7 - Dudley's Club

Much was still discussed in Parliament nowadays, in the full glare of television cameras. Committees enquired and The Lords revised. Interviews were given by ministers and fact-finding tours conducted. Votes were taken and legislation enacted. To all intents and purposes, decisions were made within the open confines of a transparent, democratic system. The reality, however, was that most decisions had already been made long before by the powerful grandees of each party in one of London's gentleman's clubs. Which club varied only slightly with a change of ruling party. Of all the plush locations for the exercise of true power, none was more effective than Dudley's Club in St James Street.

....

As a result of his performance on the floor of the House, Brian Smithe was not surprised to get an invitation to morning coffee with The Chief Whip and the Prime Minister's Parliamentary Private Secretary the following day; an invitation which suggested they meet at Dudley's Club at eleven.

The next day, at ten to eleven Brian entered Dudley's and informed the porter that he had an appointment with Sir Crispin Jessop and Sir Geoffrey Stanning.

The porter nodded and said, "This way please, Minister."

Brian Smithe, Government Minister for Families, found himself being led past at least a dozen busts of former Prime Ministers who had all been members of Dudley's. They were ranged along the main hallway and then up the staircase that led to a large lounge full of leather chairs. The Chief Whip was sitting on one of these chairs already having coffee with Sir Geoffrey Stanning. Both men looked up as Brian came into view and he was invited to join them. Sir Geoffrey poured him a cup of coffee and enquired whether he took sugar or not. Cream had been added automatically. Brian admitted he took two and was given two lumps from the dish.

"The Prime Minister felt you were a bit off form yesterday in The House and asked me to make sure you were okay," said Sir Geoffrey getting straight to the point.

"It didn't help being given the wrong figures from DWP a month back. That does make it a little difficult to try and look like we were on top of this issue when we are not."

"That may be true, but it is important that ministers put up a show whatever position they find themselves in, and quite frankly, you failed to lay a glove on the Harpie yesterday. There isn't anything preying on your mind is there?"

"No, I just had a bad day at the office. That's all," said Brian, still annoyed at having been given incorrect information by another department.

"It is important that our ministers look capable in any exchanges at the despatch box," continued Sir Geoffrey. "There are exceptions of course when the opposition have better people in place, but we had rather hoped that was restricted to Education and Overseas Development at the moment. The Prime Minister is keen that we are not out-performed on Families as well."

"This is rather a vote winner or loser for the parties at the moment and we need to know this issue is in safe hands," added Sir Crispin.

"I'm on it," said Brian. "Just tell Barry to give me the correct facts the next time from his department."

"I'm afraid Barry had to massage the facts a month ago to allow the PM to dodge a bullet from our favourite Red Top," Sir Crispin continued. "Whether his figures stacked up or not, we need to know you can deal with it in the future. The Harpie started to look competent yesterday and we can't have that."

"Are you sure there isn't anything distracting you at this exact moment in time? We can help, you know, with most situations," enquired Sir Crispin.

Brian recognised the game he was playing. If you have a problem, tell the whips what it is and they will make it go away but thereafter they own you. Sir Crispin had asked in such a way to suggest that he already knew about Susan and the twins but was allowing lee-way for an admission. Brian doubted if he did know but wasn't 100 percent sure. If he admitted that the governments 'minister for single mums' had created yet another while trying to vilify them all then he was under their thumb from that moment on. If he didn't, then he had no idea how he was going to keep Sue out of the papers. For now, she believed he was going to leave his wife and family for her. Once she realised that was a non-starter she could do anything. He did need help but wasn't sure if the Chief Whip and the PPS to the Prime Minister were his best option. Before he could make up his mind, it was made up for him.

"Success in the whip's office is based on, not what you know, but on what you know about who you know. There is a, no-doubt scurrilous, rumour doing the rounds that you have a young lady in tow, as it were," said Sir

Crispin. "Not a career stopper as such in normal circumstances; however, for the Minister for families it would look bad if it came to light. It is preferable that MPs and ministers in particular lead a life which, in public at least, resembles what you might call a Snow White Scenario: pure and unadulterated. Is there any truth in the rumour, Brian?"

For a second Brian thought he knew how the whips got their name as he felt the painful probe into his private life sting more than a little. So the bastards knew, did they? That was what this was all about. It had nothing to do with his performance against the Harpie the day before. Nobody could have defended the erroneous figures he had been given. They knew about Sue and they wanted something in return for buying his silence.

"I suspect you know there is, Sir Crispin or I wouldn't be here, would I?" said Brian.

"Don't misunderstand our motives Brian. We are keen to help you manage this situation. We have extensive experience of minimising the damage our colleagues inflict on themselves," said Sir Geoffrey. "There are always quiet solutions, and fortunately funds are never a problem for our party. Some of our supporters have very deep pockets."

"So the PM knows, does he?" Brian asked in a now worried manner.

"My dear boy," said Sir Geoffrey, " Our job is to make sure the Prime Minister only knows about situations like this when he needs to. At this exact moment in time it is the last thing he needs to know. He trusts Crispin and me to decide what he does and doesn't need to know so that if your predicament becomes public he can rightly be shocked and surprised and take whatever difficult decision has to be taken. For the moment this problem is strictly entre nous as it were."

Brian was not entirely convinced that the PM would not have been made aware of the fact that his Minister for Families had created an extra family outwith his matrimonial home. If these two knew his secret, however, he had to play their game or be sacked.

"So what exactly is your understanding of my situation," he asked.

"Our understanding is that a woman in her late twenties gave birth to twins, fathered by yourself, eight months ago and that you have been keeping her out of sight, at considerable expense, ever since. Is this true?"

"Yes," admitted Brian, seeing no point in lying.

"We need to know your intentions in this matter."

“You mean, are they honourable?” Brian snorted.

“I think we can safely rule that out,” countered Sir Crispin. “We assume you are going to remain with your wife and children and not give them up for this girl Sue.”

“That is correct,” said Brian, feeling a pang of guilt as he sold Sue out for the sake of his political career.

“Good man,” said Sir Geoffrey with a degree of sincerity. “The nick-name for your post may be the Minister for Unmarried Mothers, but you should not take your work home, as it were. There are a number of options open to us as a team to solve this problem. Does this young lady expect anything of you apart from financial support?”

“I don’t quite understand,” said Brian.

“Have you promised her your undying love etc. etc. and that you will leave your wife?" asked Sir Crispin impatiently.

“No, nothing like that,” lied Brian. “She will be happy to have some sort of permanent financial security.”

“Good, money we can arrange; undying love is beyond our remit,” said Sir Geoffrey. “I suggest you give us an address and phone number where we can arrange for somebody to contact her. You have until Monday to let her know how things are going to go. This conversation today was limited to your performance in Parliament as far as anyone must know. This other matter was never discussed. Understand? After that you must forget about her and get on with the job of neutralising The Harpie's outbursts in Parliament and in the press. Do we have a clear agreement?"

Brian found himself fixed by both men with stares which could have held the Star Ship Enterprise in a fixed orbit. He knew there was no going back after this, but they had basically offered to look after Sue and the twins for life and he could hardly turn the offer down, even if that were an option. They would own him from that moment onwards but to succeed he would have to toe the line anyway. He would still have to convince Sue that never seeing each other again would be for the best. A text might not be appropriate for that one but he would try to agree things by phone.

"We do, Sir Geoffrey," he finally said.

"Good; leave everything to us. Don't feel obliged to stay and make small talk if you have other matters to address," added Sir Crispin.

Brian knew he had been dismissed from the Headmaster's study after a caning and rose to leave. As he did so, Sir Geoffrey spoke again.

"Oh, there is one more thing. We will expect you to stop publically criticising Under-Occupancy Legislation from The Welfare Reform Act 2012."

Brian paused. 'The bastards don't waste any time do they,' he thought to himself.

"You mean the Bedroom Tax?" he replied.

"Stick with Welfare Reform, it sounds better. Remember it is designed to resolve under-occupancy; Nothing more. We made it the law; therefore it is a good thing. Reality and Politics are very different things. If you accept the party whip you must never confuse the two. Goodbye, Brian."

Brian walked out of The Dudley Club with as much dignity as he could muster; which wasn't much. He had sold himself and Sue out. From here on in he was a Party man whether he liked it or not and would have to toe the line whatever he felt regarding any legislation. He felt far worse about this than the prospect of never seeing Sue or the twins again. They both knew it had only been a fling which had gone wrong. At least he hoped they both knew it.

Once he had left the table the two senior party officials exchanged looks.

“A woman?” began Sir Crispin. “It had to be a woman with a Grammar School boy, didn’t it, and women have such a dreadful habit of getting pregnant.”

“Don’t judge everyone by your own preferences, Crispin, we’re not all frustrated old queens.”

“Oh, of course I forgot about your little problem when you were a new MP. What was that girl’s name? Natalie, Naomi…..?”

“Nicola, actually,” corrected Sir Geoffrey, a little uncomfortably.

“Whatever happened to her and her child; your child?”

“She died shortly after the child was born, I’m afraid, a hit and run. Her parents, who were ill, arranged for the child to be adopted anonymously. I never heard a thing after the local papers lost interest.”

“Best all round, really,” said Sir Crispin without a trace of feeling.

“I did love Nicola at the time, you know. The child would be a grown woman of twenty-something now. Almost thirty, come to think of it”

“Don’t dwell on it, Geoffrey. I’m sure she is doing just fine now. She came from good stock after all. Let’s focus on young Brian’s current problem, shall we?”

“What do you propose we do about her?”

“Well, let’s see if she is likely to keep quiet or not,” said Sir Crispin. “I’ll ask the usual people to monitor the situation and resolve it as they see fit. I’ll suggest they don’t wait too long to make a decision. A woman scorned and all that.”

Sir Geoffrey nodded vaguely, as if lost in his own thoughts.

Chapter 8 - Dawn Harper

When Dawn Harper won her seat in parliament from the Lib-Dem Incumbent it made headlines in an otherwise fairly predictable general election. It should have raised alarm bells amongst anyone who expected her to arrive at the Palace of Westminster as a typical star-struck newbie, overawed by the history and the pomp of her new place of work. After all, the whole place was designed to overawe all new arrivals and encourage them to blend in without rocking any boats. That was what the establishment had come to expect and with good reason. They hadn't reckoned on Dawn's determination and ability.

Instead of arriving at her office like a child on her first day at school she entered parliament like a paratrooper clearing a building of the enemy room by room. The political graveyards were full of men who had called her love or dearie, and the awkward squad of government MPs found her able to give as good as she got from day one. In the early days of her first parliamentary term the bars would be full in the evenings of her male colleagues licking their wounds after debates or committee hearings.

God help any of the old school windbags who were sent to filibuster legislation when she was about. If she didn't bludgeon them into submission in public their lives would be a misery the first chance she had to catch them elsewhere.

Most of this attitude stemmed from one thing; Dawn was not in politics for her own benefit, something which made her standout from the rest of itself. She was there as a champion of every underdog she had ever met along the way who had been shafted by somebody in power or by the system itself. Every encounter she had in life with somebody who had got on because of privilege or patronage was personal, and she hated to lose. Not through pride but because if she lost an argument to somebody like that she had failed in her duty to the downtrodden. If she did, then why was she even there?

It became clear to her very quickly that doing battle with life's privileged would be a daily struggle. Not every MP had come from a wealthy background or gone to an expensive school, but one way or another most were there for reasons other than altruism. Many may have started out in politics to help others but the system in place corrupted them very quickly into helping themselves. For some it was a slow process but for most it was almost a three line whip to plunder the public purse from day one on a slow but inexorable journey to self-enrichment in a post-elected career in The Lords or the boardrooms of industry. Many only realised they had been corrupted by office long after it had happened, such was the subtlety with which the establishment operated. A minority of new MPs were millionaires when elected but the majority were by the time they left parliament and Dawn hated this fact. As a result she was despised and feared by members of both her own party and the government. Going on record when interviewed the day after the election, she stated that generally an MP's success should be judged on how little damage they had done while in office and how little they had cost the tax payer while doing it. The last thing the party leaders needed was an honest colleague who delighted in exposing the generous nature of the Westminster gravy train. Despite this or perhaps because of it she found herself a shadow minister very early in her career. Partly this was due to her unerring ability to run rings round any minister during a debate whether in parliament or on radio and TV. The other reason was that her own party leader secretly hoped she would put her foot in it big time and he could retire her to the backbenches at the first possible opportunity. To everyone's disappointment, however, Dawn proved sure footed on every occasion.

Thus it was that she found herself up against Brian Smithe, Minister for Families, in any debate connected to his brief. Of all the people in the Cabinet at the time nobody illustrated the problem with the system better than Smithe. He looked the part and was photogenic but beyond that he was a self-seeking yes-man of the first order. He had arrived at Westminster wide-eyed and envious of the easy wealth and power of many of his senior colleagues. As a result he was exactly what they were looking for. He voted along party lines without question and would turn cart-wheels for the least hint at a slice of further power or advancement. The whips' office loved him, as they could tick him off as a 'yes' on their list, whatever vote was being discussed.

Dawn loved him because she could outclass him in a debate day in and day out. Whatever policy was being trotted out as an excuse to cut benefits or reduce assistance to 'her people' as she saw it, she could quickly expose it for the heartless, self-serving trick it was. The press loved her because of her clarity of thought and her ability to produce pithy quotes to order, her own or those of others. It could be such good pantomime that viewing figures for televised debates in parliament would be measurably higher if 'The Harpie' was due to get her teeth into Smithe or indeed anybody else who tried to out-debate her. Very soon, few tried and Brian Smithe was lined up as cannon fodder by the government on a regular basis, grateful that as yet she did not hold one of the more important portfolios. Ever grateful for the trappings of office, the hapless Smithe would dutifully turn out regularly for a mauling, looking increasingly like a keen schoolboy boxer who had been put into the ring with Mike Tyson due to some administrative error along the way.

Chapter 9 – Remembrance of Times Past

Sir Crispin left Dudley's after the meeting with Brian for some important but unspecified business. This left Sir Geoffrey on his own and, unusually for him, without a pressing engagement. The mention of Nicola's name had brought back memories which he had hoped were buried too deep to ever surface again. In the usual hurly burly of his busy day this would have been true; but here, alone with an hour to himself he failed to prevent her face re-appearing in his mind's eye.

He had loved Nicola more than he had ever loved anyone before or since. His marriage had been for all the right reasons on paper: title, money and influence, but there had never been much in the way of love. When he was campaigning for the seat he had now held for almost thirty years, his wife had been the ideal companion on the hustings. She was tall, but not quite taller than he was, beautiful in a classical way which was reminiscent of royalty and horses, and had a stock of clever remarks which she could trot out on just the right occasion to amuse people but without the strong personality to eclipse her husband. Her strongest quality, as a politician's wife though, was her amazing memory for names and faces. As Sir Geoffrey and his wife Marilyn approached any group of people in almost any important situation, she could whisper details to her husband of who they were and why they were important or not as the case may be. With Sir Geoffrey's looks and schooling and his wife's unerring knowledge of the great and good, they made a formidable team.

It wasn't until the later stages of that first campaign when Sir Geoffrey was asked by central office to take on an intern by the name of Nicola Mason, that he ever started to have doubts about how happy his marriage might actually be. On paper, Nicola was no match for Marilyn in terms of looks, background or usefulness and yet there had been something about her that Geoffrey found infectious. It was her humour he realised later. Marilyn could come out with witticisms whenever they were required or appropriate but they were all the gems of other people. She could quote Oscar Wilde or Winston Churchill and even Groucho Marx, but she lacked the spontaneous wit of any of them.

Nicola on the other hand was the most amusing person Geoffrey knew. She had nick names for everyone in politics, many of which would have horrified the person concerned and got her the sack, but she didn't seem to care. She was a rebel, a dissident and refused to pretend to be anything else. If she upset somebody she could always manage to make them laugh immediately and defuse the situation. Within the confines of Geoffrey's campaign team and the wider world of politics that made her a breath of fresh air.

Towards the end of the election campaign Marilyn had gone down with a bout of flu and had had to rest despite trying for days to struggle on at Geoffrey's side. He had admired her commitment but after she fainted at an important local debate, he had to insist that she take to her bed and focus on her health. Without his trusty encyclopaedia at his side Geoffrey struggled at first with the names and roles of many of the minor party officials he met on a daily basis. On one such occasion he had just insulted a major financial backer of the party when Nicola had made a joke of it in a way his wife could never have done. Everyone laughed and the situation was saved. Geoffrey made a point of keeping Nicola close by and was impressed at her way with people at all levels of the populace, not just the traditional Conservative voters.

On a visit to a local factory, a major employer in the area where the general workforce would be anything but supportive of a local Tory candidate, Nicola had taken it on herself to introduce him to the assembled masses in the canteen with such a relaxed and witty style that he found his own words more warmly received than he could ever have imagined. After three days with Nicola at his side he found his party's canvassing returns improve. He no longer appeared to be an also-ran but was pulling level with his Liberal Democrat rival. Central Office took note and his seat went from unlikely to marginal on their planning board.

On the evening of the election, with Marilyn in bed with pneumonia, the rest of Geoffrey's team assembled at the main vote count with a sense of excitement they had not dared to dream of at the outset of the campaign. It was possible, just possible, that this new kid on the block could steal the seat of the incumbent Lib-Dem MP.

The vote was close but after two recounts the returning officer announced that Geoffrey Stanning had been duly elected by the margin of just 78 votes. The pattern was mirrored in a number of other seats and the party began a night of celebrations as they clung on to power, if only just. Sir Geoffrey's team headed back to his campaign office and opened bottle after bottle of champagne. He even received a telephone call from the Prime Minister, congratulating him on his excellent victory. By the early hours everyone was drunk but euphoric and in no mood to end the party.

Marilyn had phoned from what sounded like a death bed and told Geoffrey she was delighted but too weak to join him.

“Lap it up with your people,” was her parting comment. “They deserve it, and I need to be ready for Westminster.”

He told her loved her, which he did, and then hung up.

"Mind you," he thought to himself, "I loved pretty much everyone at that exact moment in time."

No one more so than Nicola who he realised had helped in his victory more than most and perhaps enough to swing the swing voters his way. He told her so towards the end of the festivities and she smiled back. As their eyes met in a mildly drunken haze they both decided there was only one proper way to celebrate the occasion.

Chapter 10 – Post Erection Hangover

The morning after becoming an MP, Geoffrey Stanning woke up in the bed of one of his campaign team with a mild hangover. As he awoke, however, he realised that he had made the potentially biggest mistake of his eight hour old political career. Nicola woke around the same time too and fortunately for Geoffrey spoke first.

"You better not be found here, sweetheart. The press would crucify you before you had a chance to make your maiden speech."

Then she laughed that infectious, beautiful laugh which Geoffrey found irresistible. He kissed her tenderly and said, "I'd better go."

She nodded and laughed again but in a soft way which meant no harm. Then he showered and left her apartment, grateful that there were no paparazzi waiting outside, and went home to his sick wife. Thereafter he got on with the business of being a new MP and tried desperately hard not to think of Nicola.

He found himself lost on a steep learning curve which distracted his attention for most of his waking moments. Marilyn recovered and took her rightful place at his side. As a direct result his unfailing ability to know names and backgrounds of people as he met them returned. He made a maiden speech which drew praise from the right quarters and he was marked down in the whips' notebooks as one to watch for the future. Before he knew it months had passed and he no longer felt like a new boy when he arrived each day at The Palace of Westminster. Instead he felt like he belonged in its comfortable, old boy surroundings. He had almost, but not quite, forgotten about Nicola when his researcher shattered his new world one day.

"I see that Nicola girl Head Office sent us for the election campaign has a bun in the oven."

"What?" asked Geoffrey.

"She's due sometime about now. Apparently she had an occasional boyfriend who spends most of his time climbing mountains around the world but happened to be about at the time of the election. One night of passion and she finds herself pregnant with his sprog but by then he has buggered off to the Himalayas again. She was really funny about the whole thing, saying the child would be safer with her dad hanging from a precipice rather than hanging around the house trying to change nappies. I wondered if she was just putting on a brave face. It won't be easy bringing up a kid without a proper job, although I gather her folks are at least comfortable financially and have bought the prams and cots needed. Anyway, what do you think of this debate on Europe? Be careful on this one. The PM is watching for traitors because he might not be the PM much longer if there are too many of them. My hunch is, say nothing in public either way until it's clear which way the wind is blowing."

Geoffrey had missed the new topic of the Euro-sceptics. His thoughts were all focussed on Nicola and her expected child. He and Marilyn had been trying for children but so far without success. Nicola had never mentioned a boyfriend at any stage of the election campaign. It could be true, he supposed, which would explain why she was keen for him to leave her flat the day after he was elected. He tried to convince himself of it, but failed. It just was not the open and hopelessly honest Nicola he had got to know. He suspected that there was no such boyfriend, occasional or otherwise and that he might just be the father. If so she was being incredibly loyal to him in keeping their one night of passion a secret, even if it made things very difficult for her. He had to admit that sounded more like the girl he had fallen for. She was altogether too nice for the world of politics which he had found himself adjusting to.

He quickly agreed with his researcher about everything he had just suggested, although he had little idea what it was and asked for a few minutes' privacy to phone home. The researcher nodded, surprised at his ideas all being accepted so readily and also surprised at being excluded from the room when Geoffrey phoned Marilyn. He knew and liked Marilyn a lot. He was sure that she in turn liked him and he felt, well, almost part of the family. It didn't much matter though. After all, Geoffrey had agreed with his entire strategy for the current conflicts within the party and that had to be a good thing.

As soon as he was alone, Geoffrey phoned the phone number he had for Nicola's flat and heard her answer after a pause.

"Hello," came her unmistakable voice but without the lively enthusiasm he had known before.

"Nicola, it's me, Geoffrey. I'm sorry I haven't kept in touch. I just heard your news. How are you?"

"Fine, really fine," she said, in an obvious attempt to lie. "You just caught me actually. I'm moving back to my parents in a few days. Probably best really. They've been super about everything, apart from asking about the mountaineering boyfriend I invented."

"I have to do something. I take it she's mine?"

"Of course she's yours, Geoffrey, which is why you mustn't do anything. You are doing so well. Just don't let your party be too harsh on single mothers. They have a habit of picking on them." She laughed at her joke and Geoffrey pictured her as she had been when he last saw her in her flat.

"What about money? I want to help. I have to do something."

"You already have. You've given me a beautiful daughter. Now get back to work." Again she laughed and Geoffrey felt a stab at his heart.

"When is she due?" he asked.

"She was born three days ago, Dozy. You've been an MP for nine months now, or have you been too busy to notice?"

"I suppose I have really. I feel dreadful now. What have you called her?"

"I haven't decided yet but I'll come up with something suitable. Now get back to work. We'll be fine."

With that the line went dead and when Geoffrey rang again there was no answer. He never spoke to Nicola again. Some months later he heard that she had been hit by a car while pushing her child in a pram. The car had struck with force and failed to stop. By a miracle the child was unharmed despite severe damage to the pram itself. His researcher gathered the child had been put up for adoption due to the grandparents' ill health, greatly exacerbated by their daughter's death.

Thereafter Geoffrey buried himself in his work and tried desperately to drive the memory of Nicola and their child from his thoughts. This had been helped some years later when Marilyn gave birth to a son, followed in successive years by a further three boys; girls were rare in both Geoffrey's and Marilyn's families. Like buses, after waiting years for a child, four came along one after another.

His career blossomed too and he held several key junior ministerial posts before being appointed as Environment secretary. He was briefly appointed to the whips' office but found the work 'grubby' and distasteful. When he said so in the wrong places he was moved to Secretary of State for Wales as a punishment in the next reshuffle; a move justified on the basis of a distant Welsh aunt who had written books about Welsh wild flowers. He became rather popular in this post and with the country as a whole so that years later he was seen as a suitable avuncular figure to oversee the early years in power of a rather young Prime Minister. As Parliamentary Private Secretary he was far from the usual up and coming young man in this post, but his presence at the side of an inexperienced PM sat well with voters. It also allowed the party Grandees to influence the PM's activities when necessary.

In this post he became very influential and regularly dealt with Sir Crispin and his team of whips. He saw them at best as a necessary evil now but still grubby and perhaps dangerous individuals.

Left alone in Dudley's that morning following the meeting with Sir Crispin his thoughts had wandered back in time and over his career since entering Parliament and he was not convinced he had done his best. "Would Nicola have approved?" he wondered. Had he become hardened and corrupted? Almost certainly. As badly as Crispin? Heaven forbid. Crispin was born evil.

Chapter 11 - Double Booked

The transit van and the Range Rover arrived at the Mews property around midnight. In a slick series of movements which required no spoken words and only a few hand signals, the vehicles were reversed quietly into the double garage and the doors closed over. Only then did the men in the rear seats of the vehicles emerge, all carrying heavy duty grips and rucksacks. One unlocked the door which connected the garage and the kitchen and each man in turn made his way through the door and onwards to the living room. Once there, they put the heavy luggage down and waited. Only when the final one of the nine entered the room and all curtains in the downstairs rooms had been securely shut was a light put on in the living room.

At a signal from the man in charge, two of the group made their way to the bottom of the staircase. As they got there they heard a noise coming from upstairs. Both took pistols from concealed holsters and looked round at their boss for guidance. He indicated for them to halt for a second and everyone listened carefully to see if the noise was repeated. After a minute or so it was but this time louder and was more distinct. The man in charge moved forward to join his colleagues at the bottom of the stairs. The noise was repeated a third time and on this occasion was clearly the sound of a young child or baby crying.

The three men looked at each other in surprise. The leader signalled that he would go first and the other two should follow but indicated first to re-holster their weapons. As they reached the top landing the sound came again, obviously now a child and clearly coming from the second door along. The senior figure made his way to the door and, with the two ready to back him up with whatever they found, he burst through the doorway switching the light on as he went.

Inside was a bedroom with four institutional style metal beds crammed in. On top of the one nearest the hall was a Moses basket with a baby in it. The baby was awake and looked at the startled men. Then it started crying without pause. It was also stinking, as only babies with full nappies can.

From one of the other rooms came a woman's voice: "All right, all right, I'm coming."

The largest of the men was dispatched to meet her in the corridor and to keep her quiet. The leader of the group indicated to the remaining soldier to check out the first room. As Sue came out of the smallest bedroom, still tying her dressing gown, she found herself facing a dark, monstrous figure in the corridor. Before she could let out the scream which was forming in her throat she was grabbed and picked up by two massive arms which felt like vices. She kicked and wrestled with all her strength but found it a useless exercise. With a hand over her mouth she could make no sound even when another dark figure appeared out of the first bedroom carrying Joe. When she saw this she kicked and struggled, digging her heels into the legs of the man who held her. He didn't seem to feel a thing.

A third figure appeared from Ben's bedroom and walked up to her face where she could see him, even in the gloom. He put a finger to his lips and lent over to her ear.

"We won't hurt you or the kids but you must keep quiet; understood?" said a deep and commanding voice that suggested it would be best to comply.

The hand holding her head loosened just enough for her to nod slightly and she felt the grip of both arms slowly release her. The arms stayed around her, though, ready to subdue her again if she made a noise. She didn't dare, but her maternal instincts gave her the courage, as soon as she was released, to rush over to the figure holding the still sleeping Joe and prise him out of the stranger's hands.

For a second Sue stood there just staring at the man who had held her child while the three men stared at her, equally surprised at the turn of events but not in any way terrified. After a long pause, the man who had spoken before whispered.

“Who the fuck are you?”

“I live here. Who the fuck are you?”

This seemed to set him thinking. He signalled for the giant to lead her into the room where Ben was still crying, so that all three of them were together, then disappeared down stairs with the third man. Sue gently placed Joe down on one of the beds and picked up Ben. Glancing at the man who had grabbed her and was now apparently her jailer she undid her nightdress and started to breast feed the hungry child. She was relieved to see that the large man walked over to the door and partly turned away from her as she did so. He did look back every few minutes but only to reassure himself that she was staying put and not in any voyeuristic way. At least he is human, she thought.

Downstairs a group of seven men stood in a huddle round their leader.

“Right, lads,” he said quietly. “We have company upstairs.”

One of the men took a pistol from his pocket at this news.

"You won't need that," said his boss firmly. "There seems to be a squatter in the house; a woman with two kids. She said she lives here but this is the correct address and all the keys have worked. There are only a few things belonging to her and the kids, and the bedrooms are all kitted out as before. I did a recce here a year ago. I'm going to find out who the fuck she is and decide what we do with her. John the Beast is keeping her in place so she may have died of fright by now anyway. The rest of you sort yourselves out here and in the kitchen. We are still on eight hours' notice to move so chill for now. Mac, you stay here now, I'll sort this out."

"Right Boss," came the reply from the group, and the oldest of the group started tasking the men while his boss went back upstairs.

When he reached the bedroom where Sue was huddled with her kids he told his huge colleague to wait outside and walked in to speak to her. He found her sitting on the edge of one of the barrack room beds, breast- feeding one baby while resting one hand on the other infant lying beside her. He made no apology but also conveyed no immediate threat.

"Who are you, and why are you in this property?" he asked her in a calm voice.

There was a firmness and confidence in his voice which Sue noted, but despite this she thought only of the safety of her children and tried to bluff an answer.

"I live here and have no intention of answering your questions. Either you leave or I will phone the police."

The man stared at her unmoved then handed her his phone, "On you go. 999 should get them."

Sue took the phone out of sheer bravado but when she saw that he was prepared to let her dial the police she gave up and handed it back.

"Who are you?" she asked meekly after he took the phone and put it back in his pocket.

"That is none of your business. We should be here and you should not. I suggest you tell me who you are immediately."

Sue stared into his face looking for a hint of compassion or weakness but found none.

"I'm Sue, Sue White, and I was placed here by the Government, so you'd better be careful."

The man was again completely unmoved at this news.

"Which department?" he asked.

"Families Ministry," she answered confidently.

“You know this isn’t a fucking council house, don’t you?” the man asked impatiently.

“I was placed here by the Families Department and have every right to be here,” replied Sue trying desperately to sound confident.

“This property is under the control of The Home Office and you have no right to be here. Give me the contact details of the person who placed you in this house and I will resolve this, but you should not be here. Get your things ready to move.”

Sue thought for a second about Brian, and even David who had been so kind, and decided she had to maintain her silence.

“I am not prepared to say any more to you,” was all she managed to say.

The man stared at her.

“I will now contact the Families Department and make sure whoever gave you a key to this place is out of work by lunchtime tomorrow. Wait here.”

As the man stood up to leave, clearly meaning every word of what he had said, Sue weakened.

“No wait. Don’t do that.”

The man stopped and turned towards her,

“Give me one good reason why I shouldn’t”

“I don’t want any trouble for the father of my children.”

“Who is he?” asked the man.

“That’s classified,” said Sue.

A brief raised eyebrow was followed by the man walking away unimpressed.

“Bugger,” Sue hissed under her breath, worried that she was about to land Brian in it.

Downstairs the senior figure signalled to the oldest of the group to follow him into the kitchen. Once they reached the utility room he turned.

“There is a woman with two small kids, probably twins, squatting in this house. She claims she was placed here by the Families Ministry but won’t give me the name of who placed her here. She turned down the option of phoning the police so she must have something to hide. The way I see it we have two options; neither of them great. We can contact police liaison and have her taken away, in which case our cover is blown as Plod will immediately tell all his mates we're here, or we can hold her here, in which case we are effectively taking a hostage while on anti-hostage duty. Any ideas?”

"Tough one, Boss," said the Sergeant Major. "If we hand her over to the police our cover will be blown for sure. The senior brass in the Met hate The Regiment since we sorted The Iranian Embassy siege, half the armed officers in The Met claim they are part of the Regiment and most of them would sell the story that we are here to the press and retire. Bottom line is we can't trust the police to keep our presence here a secret. If she was a terrorist or something we could deal with that quietly ourselves but she obviously isn't and if anyone threatens her kids I'll kill them personally. Best bet is we keep her here till we can place her somewhere without Old Bill finding out. Probably get one of our own to remove her to another safe house meantime. Any idea who the father is?"

"No idea. I don't even know for certain if she knows, but I agree on your appreciation of the problem. Come with me."

The two men headed back up stairs and relieved the guard at Sue's door, who headed downstairs to join the rest. They walked calmly into the bedroom where Sue was still trying to breast -feed a now sleeping child.

"Sue, we find ourselves in an unusual but not irresolvable situation. You are here but should not be. We are here but would rather people were not fully aware of the fact. You are reluctant to go to the police, as are we, though for very different reasons, as we have every right to be here.

I suggest that you remain here while we find somewhere for you to go or we leave. In the mean time I guarantee that you and your children are quite safe. Is there anybody who could put you up somewhere without the Families Ministry or the Police being involved?"

Sue looked at him and the new, rather scarred face who had joined him, and then gave way to her emotions.

"No," she sobbed. "There is no one else I can turn to and I can't tell you why I am here."

"Okay," said the leader of the group. "Give me your mobile phone and we will take care of you and your children till we can sort something or we leave."

He held out his hand and after a few moments hesitation Sue handed him her phone. She was still crying but it was partly in relief that she and the twins appeared to be safe for the moment.

"You better," she said between the tears. "If you hurt my kids I'll kill you."

Chapter 12 - Domestic Arrangements

Once Sue had handed her phone over and accepted the situation she now found herself in, everyone relaxed visibly. The oldest of the men returned to his colleagues down stairs to brief them while the man who appeared to be in charge actually smiled.

"My name is Jason," he said. "That was Bob, Old Bob, there is another Bob downstairs, Disco Bob."

"How many of you are there?" asked Sue, having stopped crying and started wondering who her new flat mates were.

"There are nine of us here. Hopefully you won't be here long enough to get to know them. The reason we are here is none of your concern. Rest assured, we are the good guys."

"What about the big guy who grabbed me? Is he a good guy too?"

"John the Beast?" said Jason. "Yes; him too. Only just though."

Jason laughed at that and Sue joined in, mainly as a release of the fear she had felt.

"Either way, you will be quite safe here till we leave or we find somewhere safe for you to go."

"Are you bank robbers or something?" asked Sue, still at a loss to know who these men were.

"Something," said Jason as he rose and went down stairs. "I'll be back shortly and we'll sort out the small bedroom for you and the kids. We will have to get some sleep so we will need the other bedrooms. What are the twins called?"

"Ben and Joe," said Sue.

"Nice names," said Jason smiling and left the room.

Downstairs the other men were sitting around or rummaging through their bags. Old Bob had briefed them on the basic situation and they had taken it in their stride, bizarre though it was.

"We'll move the family group into the small bedroom upstairs which was for me and hot bed the other eight bunks as necessary. I don't know how long we will have to wait here but it could be a while. I'll try and sort someplace for them to go. In the meantime, show her respect and try not to scare her. The Beast nearly killed her with fright earlier and Mac holding one of her kids just about finished her off. The kid will need years of therapy too. Steve, you and Ray move her stuff. At least you two look human."

Upstairs, the three entered the bedroom where Sue was sitting with the twins.

"This is Steve and this is Ray," Jason said introducing another two new faces. "They'll help you move all your stuff into the small bedroom for now. That room will be out of bounds to troops but don't leave the building till we sort something out for you. I'll know better tomorrow how long we are likely to be here."

Sue nodded and smiled at the two newcomers. She was pleasantly surprised to see that they seemed quite normal, friendly even. Straight away they started moving the twins gently into the single bedroom, placing the cots side by side on the desk. Then they moved the associated paraphernalia of childcare, noting as they did so that this woman really didn't have much to speak of beyond the basic necessities for the children.

Once everything was moved Steve turned to her and asked if she wanted a cup of tea or coffee. Sue was now wide awake and all thoughts of more sleep that night had vanished.

"Yes please," she answered with a smile. "Coffee with milk and two sugars."

"NATO standard," said Steve.

"What?" asked Sue.

"NATO standard issue," Ray explained; "Milk and two sugars."

"Oh, I see," said Sue, still a little confused.

"Be right back," said Steve and disappeared downstairs leaving Ray in charge of small talk.

"Do you work for NATO then?"

"Yes, sort of. Some of the time at least."

"Is that what you are doing here?"

"Can't go into that," replied Ray. "If I tell you I'd have to kill you."

He smiled as he said it but it didn't fully put her mind at rest.

"Don't worry," he added. "You and the kids are safe with us."

"What about the big guy who grabbed me when you all arrived?"

Ray thought for a second, "Oh, John the Beast? You're safe from him too."

"I supposed you're going to tell me he is really just a big softy," said Sue with an element of hope in her voice.

"No, actually he's fucking lethal with a temper to match but he's on our side," said Ray before adding. "Just as well really."

"You're all soldiers, aren't you?" said Sue.

"Yeh, something like that," admitted Ray, keen not to go into any further detail.

Steve arrived with the coffee and said to Ray, "The Boss wants you downstairs."

Chapter 13 - COBRA

Sir Geoffrey Stanning ticked off the various attendees of the meeting as they arrived. The Heads of MI5, MI6 and QCHQ had arrived with him from Dudley's. The press loved to report these meetings as COBRA, short for Cabinet Office Briefing Room A but on this occasion it was being held in room B; room A being in the process of getting a fresh coat of paint. Those attending tended to simply refer to it as 'The Briefing Room'.

The Head of the Army was first to arrive followed by the Commissioner of The Metropolitan Police who arrived with the Commander of SCO19, The Metropolitan Police Specialist Firearms Command. The Defence Secretary and the Home Secretary arrived together and were followed shortly afterwards by the Commanding Officer of The Special Air Service who looked over at the Commander of SCO19 and shrugged his shoulders as if to say: "Don't blame me for this." The Chief Fire Officer for Central London arrived as did the director of Medical services and a few other civil servants. Once Sir Geoffrey's list was complete he sent a text and two minutes later The Prime Minister arrived with his press officer.

The PM sat down and immediately welcomed everyone and thanked them for making time for this in their busy schedules. The fact that they had no choice but to be there was ignored.

"You will all know from the briefing notes you received that The Security Service and GCHQ have uncovered plans for a 'Spectacular' to take place in London over the next two months. They have identified six members of the plot and their handlers overseas. Unfortunately five of the group have fallen off the radar, leaving all their phones and laptops in their respective accommodation throughout the country. Our only link now is via the Quarter Master of the Group who has remained in Glasgow. He had not been in direct contact with the others but communicated only via a single point of contact in Pakistan and then using the Dark Web or The Onion Router on an occasional basis. He believes that his cover is intact but we have managed to confirm that the hardware he has been guarding is also still in Glasgow."

"Are we 100% sure of this?" The Commissioner of The Met interrupted.

"Yes," the head of MI5 confirmed simply.

"How?" asked The Commissioner.

“Without going into detail,” said the head of MI5 with a hint of annoyance in his voice, “because we have eyes on it.”

“It would be better if we all allow the PM to finish his summary,” said Sir Crispin Jessop in a way that sounded like career advice for all those present.

“Thank you, Crispin,” said the PM. “I know that all the agencies responsible for security in London have been working closely together to try to find the missing five, but as yet they have not succeeded. The Home Secretary recently increased the Threat Level to Severe, as you know. As an additional precaution I have ordered a team from The Special Air Service Regiment, Special Projects Team to stand by to assist.”

The Commissioner of the Met again interrupted, aware that he was already at the top of his career with less than a year to go and sanctions were limited in his case.

“The Met currently has almost three thousand qualified firearms officers available with SCO19 ready and trained (largely by the SAS) to deal with any situation within the rule of law. I would like to think we would be allowed to proceed on that basis without the use of a hit squad. There is still police primacy in this country I assume.”

The Prime Minister looked visibly annoyed at this and was about to answer when his press secretary did so for him.

“The team from the SAS is here to assist the police if required and to reassure the country as a whole that they are safe from terrorists, whatever it may take. We will be releasing a press bulletin shortly to ask the public to remain vigilant and to put their minds at rest. We can’t have panic in the run up to a general election.”

“If I understand," continued the Commissioner, "the SAS team is already in London but I have not been informed and you are about to tell the press as much? Every journalist in Britain will be trying to track them down for a scoop instead of looking for the terrorists. I wouldn’t be cynical enough to suggest the impending election was a factor in the decision-making process. At what stage was I going to be informed of their presence, assuming they are indeed falling under my command?”

Sir Crispin made a quiet note at this point, perhaps about early gardening leave for the head of the Met, who already appeared to be demob happy, going by his line of questioning.

“You are being informed of the SAS presence now and in tandem with my department you will be able to call on them as you see fit,” added the Home Secretary who was obviously more used to working with the Commissioner's approach to politics.

"Thank you, Home Secretary," said the PM. "We are all on the same side and must ensure the safety of the public. For that reason we must locate the five missing members of this cell as quickly as possible, even if it means we have to allow the sixth member to leave Glasgow and join them. If we simply arrest him now we will allow the others to remain loose with the possibility of reforming around a different plan. If we do find them then their associate in Scotland will be immediately taken into custody. I have another meeting to chair so I expect this group to work together from here on in, under the chairmanship of the Home Secretary, to ensure that we catch these people and reduce the threat level in time for the General Election."

Chapter 14- Commissioner of Police of the Metropolis

Michael 'Iron Mike' Steel

Commissioner Michael 'Iron Mike' Steel hated politicians. It was only fair after all; he hated everyone. Hated was perhaps too strong a word for his feelings towards his fellow man. Everyone broke the law to a greater or lesser extent, and that made them all criminals. Mike had devoted his life to catching criminals and making the world a safer and more orderly place. Politicians broke the laws that they themselves had made, and that made them hypocrites and criminals. But his distaste for politicians ran much deeper than that.

As a young detective sergeant he had been involved in a stake-out watching a house in west London where several men were known to abuse young boys. For Mike that made them the lowest of the low. He knew that every real villain he had ever put away agreed and that once these perverts went to jail their lives wouldn't be worth living. Hardened criminals would take out their anger and frustration on 'nonces' as if it were a sacred duty and the prison guards would be under- zealous about stopping them.

After three long and boring months of watching and photographing the comings and goings from the guest house it was discovered that one of the regular visitors was a government whip. Mike and his colleagues had had a good laugh at that one; in the days when Mike still laughed. He reported the visits of this individual, expecting the team to move in and arrest all concerned at the first opportunity. Instead the whole investigation was stopped the next morning. Mike and his colleagues were called in to a briefing room and told by their chief inspector that the investigation was over. He thanked them for their hard work through gritted teeth and told them they would be reassigned during the course of the day. When the briefing was finished Mike collared his boss and objected.

"We've got these bastards by the short and curlies, including the MP."

"That's why we've been stood down, Mike. Some people are above the law, Mike. Get used to it or get another job."

Mike went through a long period of soul-searching after that. He could leave as a matter of principle but then what would he do? He had always wanted to be a copper and no other job would do. He could refuse to give up the current investigation and try and nick the men the team had been monitoring. This option would be career-threatening at the very least, and by the sound of the instruction from his boss he would get nowhere with it: these people were protected by contacts at the very top of the pile. The third option was the easiest on the face of it; he would remain a copper and try to deal with it as he put away as many other villains as possible. Eventually and reluctantly he opted for the last of these options and threw himself into his career.

Mike grew up a lot that day and felt that he had compromised his principles ever since. His career had been built on an acceptance of that decision and as a result, of all the people he hated, he hated himself most of all.

As a result of all this he hated any time he had to spend with politicians intensely. Unfortunately for him, as Commissioner of The Metropolitan Police he had to spend a lot of time with them. No occasion was worse than the fortunately rare times he was summonsed to a COBRA meeting. Here he was locked into a room with the greatest villains he knew. He could feel them look down on him as a lackey who had turned a blind eye once and been tainted ever since. Retirement couldn't come quickly enough, although that would not bring peace. It did mean, however, that he would speak his mind on such occasions, with only the possibility of an even earlier retirement as punishment being available to his political masters.

Chapter 15 – The Press Taste Blood

Bert Butterfield had grown up wanting to be a journalist throughout most his school days. A course at college in Leeds saw him qualified for the profession and he was lucky enough to start as a junior reporter with his local paper soon afterwards, based largely on his experience of writing for the school paper and his college equivalent. The articles were of no great interest outwith the circle of his contemporaries but the editor of the newspaper recognised a tight, economic style which could be useful for filling the weekly pages under his control.

Bert spent seven years covering the local cattle market, gala days and endless school events where he had to hide his complete disinterest in what was going on and produce material which pleased both his editor and the families and friends of those involved. He hated it but realised he was serving an apprenticeship which might eventually lead to bigger and better things.

Shortly after his twenty sixth birthday he was having a few pints with one of the few school friends he had kept in touch with when he heard something of interest from a career point of view.

His friend had walked into a job with the local authority by virtue of his father already working there and had quickly found himself employed as a janitor at the town hall. Having a driving licence, he also found himself driving vehicles of various kinds as required. Eventually this included chauffeuring the Lord Provost around to functions when his regular driver was on holiday or ill. This didn't happen often but required a driver to be available for long days, which consisted mainly of waiting around outside venues where the Lord Provost was saying a few words before eating and drinking seven or eight times a day; no wonder the Provost at that time was nick-named 'Chubby'. Bert's friend had had a few pints before Bert arrived and had forgotten any requirement for discretion in his driving duties.

"You'll never guess what happened last time I had to drive Chubby around," the friend began.

He was quite correct as Bert couldn't guess what had happened. He wasn't initially sure he was interested at all. But that was about to change. He shook his head to indicate his ignorance and his friend, Kevin, continued.

"After all the events I was expecting to drive Chubby home before taking the limo back to the transport depot, but no. Guess where he asked me to take him?"

Bert was regretting meeting Kevin for a drink but somewhere in his head, his journalistic instincts told him to keep listening.

"Go on, mate," he encouraged, swithering about buying another round.

"Back to the council chambers," said Kevin with a flourish, as if he had let slip the scoop of the century.

"You took the Provost, who is a Councillor, to the council Chambers in his official council car? So fucking what?" said Bert, determined now to avoid the expense of another round and to escape as quickly as possible.

"No, you don't understand," continued Kevin. "This was 10 0'clock at night."

Bert's expressionless face suggested to Kevin that he had to get to the point.

"He had a key to let himself in, but he wasn't the only one there. The lights were already on."

"And…" coaxed Bert.

"Councillor Maybury was there already."

"So you reckon he is having an affair with Old Mrs Maybury ?" added Bert starting to show a genuine interest for the first time. "Are you sure?"

"Yes, because I have a key to the place as well and let myself in. I saw them at it in the council meeting chamber."

"Really?"

"Yes, but not Old Mrs Maybury."

"You just said it was. Make your mind up."

"I said it was councillor Maybury. But there are two; husband and wife."

It took a second for the truth to sink in fully.

"You're saying that Chubby and Tom Maybury were at it together in the Council chambers?" asked Bert after looking round to check nobody was listening in.

"Exactly!" said Kevin before going on. "Tom was wearing women's underwear and Chubby kept calling him Sally."

Bert laughed before he could stop himself.

"Honestly?" he demanded.

"Cross my heart and hope to die," confirmed Kevin.

Over the next few days Bert carried out his usual duties of attending two schools which had successfully completed road safety projects, interviewing a local florist who was retiring after 48 years in the business and he checked out the new Mobile Library bus which was inaugurated on the Thursday afternoon by The Lord Provost and his equally large wife.

The official car went on to an evening reception with the local Chamber of Commerce before it dropped off Chubby's wife at home. Bert knew this because he had followed it, as was now usual, after finishing his own assignments for the day. Shortly after ten o'clock the car arrived at the Council Chambers and Chubby let himself in while his regular driver drove round the corner to park and have a kip.

Bert waited for a few minutes and then walked over to the building. One of the windows to the Chamber itself was in a relatively dark corner and Bert made his way there carrying the small step ladder which he had started carrying around in the boot of his car.

After looking round to check that nobody was watching he set up the step ladder, climbed to the top step and looked in. The image of what he saw would stay with him for life but he was prepared enough to get his camera and record the figures inside in fairly clear detail.

Armed with his newly written article and some freshly printed photographs, he breezed into his editor's office first thing the next morning and said, "Hold the front page."

His editor looked up in surprise and then down in even greater surprise at the pictures which had been placed on his desk.

"What the fuck is this?" he shouted at Bert.

"It's the biggest scandal to hit the town for years. We'll sell double the usual number of copies and the story will run and run as they try to wriggle out of it and their marriages fall apart. We can syndicate it to the national press too. They'll love it."

"Are you mad? We don't do scandal. Now get back to work. I don't pay you to dig up dirt like this."

Bert was crestfallen. He had been sure he had the scoop of the decade at least and had pictured promotion and a pay rise on the strength of it. The last thing he had expected was a complete rejection of his 'Call me Sally' exposé.

"You have to print it," he pleaded. " The public have a right to know."

"No they don't," his boss countered immediately. "They have a right to know what's happening in the cattle market, in the schools (as long as it doesn't involve dodgy teachers) and when the new library bus will come round. They have a right to know when their bins will be emptied, when local shop-keepers retire and any changes to the bus timetables. They do not have a right to know about the private lives of local elected officials. It is none of their business and should remain so. Now get back to work. St Thomas's have won the county chess tournament for high schools and that is front page news here."

Bert was about to pick up the photographs and the draft of his article but his boss was quicker and snatched the pages up before tearing them into shreds and throwing them in the bin.

"Learn a bit of respect for important people and you'll go far in this job," shouted Bert's editor as the junior reporter trudged out of his office.

But Bert didn't go to St Thomas's to get the low-down on their massive chess achievement. Instead he went to his desk and found the contact telephone number for the city desk of one of the National Sunday papers. Fifteen minutes later he left the office of the Downfield Advertiser for the last time, having deliberately poured a full cup of coffee into his desk top computer before leaving.

Chapter 16 - House Rules

Jason gathered everyone together to brief them on the unexpected guests in the house.

"For those who haven't met her yet, we have a lady called Sue staying here with her twins, Joe and Ben. I don't know who the fuck let her in, but the fact is they are here and we cannot hand her over to the Met without them knowing where we are, which will mean the tabloids will report we are in town and we might as well go back to Hereford. Her stuff and the kids are now in the small bedroom upstairs where she will stay. It's out of bounds to troops as is she, while we are here. I'm going to try to find a way of getting her out of here without Plod getting wind of us and will see if someone else from the Regiment can be called in to help when I go to the next briefing. In the meantime nothing else has changed; we remain on eight hours' notice to move for now, as the target has not yet arrived in London. Any questions?"

"Is she fit?" asked Mac.

“Fuck off and get on with your work,” said Jason before walking over to the radio equipment.

Two of the younger men followed him and briefed him on the state of play.

“We have secure 'comms' now, up the way and down and the secure printer will be working soon,” said one of them. “We have sent a sit-rep that we are here and ready, but left out any mention of the crèche.”

“Good,” said Jason. “I want one of you stagged on with the radio from now on. Anything new, tell me straight away.”

Chapter 17 - Meet The Gang Cause the Gang's all here

When the two men had both left the room, Sue found herself alone again. She sipped the coffee and looked over at the twins who were sound asleep in their cots. She realised the men must have brought their own coffee as this cup was much better than the cheap rubbish David had left in the house with the groceries.

Once she had emptied the mug she looked round for somewhere to leave it but then thought taking it down to the kitchen would give her an excuse to see who else had arrived at the house. After she had again checked that the twins were sleeping soundly she took the mug and headed downstairs.

The lounge was a hive of activity and seemed absolutely full of people, luggage and equipment. She had heard people dropping off some things in the two larger bedrooms and guessed it must have been personal items as everything in the lounge seemed connected to war.

Two men she hadn't seen before were setting up a variety of green equipment which she decided was a radio or radios. The two looked up as she entered and nodded as if they had known her for years before resuming their activity. Sue felt hurt; she was used to at least some interest from most men. These two were either gay or very disciplined people. The Scottish soldier who had picked up Joe was sitting on one of the armchairs stripping and cleaning a shotgun. He looked up briefly and grinned but if it was meant to reassure her it failed miserably. He was wearing only a vest-like Tee-shirt on top and seemed to be constructed entirely of string and bones. Powerful looking string though. She had seen an exhibition of preserved corpses by Gunther von Hagen once and Mac looked like an exhibit who had decided to come back to life.

On the sofa a large black soldier was also cleaning a weapon. Sue wasn't sure what it was but he had a belt with what looked like grenades beside him so she assumed the two were connected. He looked up and smiled and said "Hi" in a fairly friendly manner. "I'm Bob. You must be Sue."

"Disco Bob?" asked Sue.

“Yes,” he replied. “Have we met before?”

“No,” said Sue, “But I already met Old Bob.”

“I see. I gather you know Mac here too.”

Again Mac looked up but without smiling this time; something Sue found strangely less threatening.

“The two school kids over there are ‘Debbie’ Reynolds on the left and ‘Sandy’ Shaw wearing the mop on his head.”

Sue looked over but noticed the two men had continued working away. All the men she had seen so far had very short hair or shaved heads; ‘Sandy’ Shaw was unique in having a full head of straw coloured hair. He did look very young and was of slight build compared to most of the others but she doubted he was recently out of school. The way he was setting up the equipment and his air of confidence in the company of the others suggested years of training and experience. ‘Debbie’ seemed only slightly older but in terms of looks was similar to the rest, having a crew cut and being quite broadly built

“Ray and ‘Just’ Steve helped you move house so you have probably met everyone now.”

“Is Jason in charge?”

"Yes he's the boss. That's why we all call him Boss although Old Bob runs things a lot of the time."

"Where's the big guy?" asked Sue.

"John The Beast? He's at the wagons checking them over."

"He's a bit scary but I suppose I'll get used to him."

"If you do you'll be the only one. I'm not scared of anyone but I know he'd kill me if we ever got to it."

Sue looked at Disco Bob's powerful physique and must have looked worried at Bob's comment.

Bob noticed and said, "You'll be safe enough here. We are all on duty as it were and the boss said we have to look after you and the kids. As it is spoken; so shall it be."

With that he went back to assembling and testing the grenade launcher.

Sue walked through to the kitchen where Ray and 'Just' Steve were checking small machine guns on the kitchen table.

"Hi Sue," said Ray looking up as if the two were buttering toast and reading the papers. "Kids still asleep?"

"Yep, thank God," said Sue, relieved to be with two quite ordinary looking men. "Coffees?"

"Always," said Steve. "Both with milk and two sugars, thanks."

"NATO standard," said Sue making them both smile.

The three of them sat drinking the coffees and chatting away about nothing in particular, all conscious that they had secrets to keep regarding their present set of circumstances. After half an hour or so the connecting door to the garage opened and Jason, Old Bob and John the Beast walked through.

"Everything okay?" Jason asked.

"Yes thanks," replied Sue before realising he had been asking Ray and Steve.

"Fine, Boss," said Steve.

The three men walked on and into the lounge. John was carrying a huge canvas grip which Sue thought with a shudder was big enough to hold a body. A metallic clank confirmed it didn't, much to her relief.

Chapter 18 - The Leader of Her Majesty's Opposition

Edward 'Eddie' Benton had been a member of parliament for over thirty years when, as much to his surprise as the country's, he was elected as the leader of his party. In many ways it was a rejection by his party's supporters of its occupation of the middle ground and what was seen by many as an attempt to compete on policy with the right. He had followed a very straight line in his political career which had always sat well with his former mining community constituents but less well recently with his party leaders. As a result he knew parliament and its ways inside out but had learned them from the vantage point of the back benches. He had been seen as too left of centre and principled to be a reliable member of either a cabinet or a shadow cabinet and had therefore never had to compromise the principles which had been instilled in him by his parents. He had been kept off school on occasions to take part in CND rallies and had regularly visited friends of his parents at Peace Camps at both Faslane and Greenham Common, often staying there for a few days learning how to start fires and change the world simultaneously. He had been anti apartheid since his primary school days in Leeds when future party leaders were largely disinterested in anything outwith the fashionable struggle at home. He had watched members of his party come and go over the years with many becoming corrupted and greedy by the riches available to those who were more flexible than him in their beliefs. Some had arrived with ambition for themselves rather than the world and while this upset him in his early political life, he had become less judgmental as the years went on.

When he found himself as leader of the party he found a reawakening of the zeal of his youth and looked around for younger members of the party who might be able to carry the torch after his inevitable, imminent relinquishing of power. Amongst those he found at his side, nobody embodied the spirit of his youth and indeed his parents' views more than Dawn Harper. She had missed out on the comfortable middle class upbringing he had enjoyed and her desire to help others stemmed from her difficult early years. He watched her first few years in the corridors of powers to see if she would succumb to the usual temptations of power. He was pleased to see she did not. Her expenses were modest or non-existent. On any issue wherc people were suffering at the hands of corporate greed or government political bias, she was fearless in their defence. She suffered the slings and arrows of a generally right wing press with steely resolve and a tenacious determination which he knew he had lacked as a fresher.

After his election as party leader he called in his team to form a shadow cabinet and included Dawn as a natural ally and a person to carry the flame, years into the future. When she arrived at his office he had a few options in mind but wasn't entirely surprised that she demanded the Shadow Families portfolio before he had a chance to lay out his thoughts to her. She was ready for an argument but instead he just smiled.

"I thought you might fancy that one. Would you like to know the others which I had considered you for, although that was one of them?"

"No thanks," said Dawn. "This is the one I want, for now. I have had that little shit Smithe in my sights for a while now and I want to rip him apart."

Eddie had been about to urge caution before he changed his mind and simply said: "Go get him then."

Dawn looked at his face and a smile appeared briefly on her features. There was a brief moment of connection; a passing of a baton before her face returned to its usual determined norm and she left his office at a trot.

The press had a predictable pop at every one of his appointments and Dawn's was no different. Too young, too inexperienced, too volatile too... anything they could think of. A number of female journalists were more sympathetic, welcoming the chance given to a principled young woman in the man's world of politics even if it was perhaps too soon. Only The Guardian went into raptures about his appointments, turning cartwheels in celebration at The Labour party's swing back to the left and its working class roots. It even saw its readership numbers increase briefly before continuing the descent which all papers were experiencing in the face of online competition.

Dawn lost no time in attacking her opposite number across the floor of the Commons, gaining resounding cheers from her own side and quiet admiration from her opponents who found they needed all the support they could muster in the press to neutralise the effect on the hapless Brian Smithe.

Eddie watched Dawn's progress with quiet satisfaction. He didn't cheer or jeer in the Commons as some of his colleagues tended to do. Instead he would take a fatherly pride in every blow she landed on her opponent or, on occasions, other ministers who foolishly took her on in a debate. He watched with interest as she contributed at meetings of his shadow cabinet and tried to temper her attacks on colleagues gently to improve her ability to work as a member of a team without diluting her enthusiasm for their shared cause.

For the Government's part, Dawn was picked up as a threat very early on their radar. Brian was deliberate cannon fodder as far as the leadership was concerned. The policies he had to implement were always going to be unpopular with a lot of people and there was no point in having anybody valuable in that portfolio until all the necessary bad news had been delivered and he could be dispensed with. He was bright enough to realise it and might have done so if he had not had the ego and arrogance to believe his success was in some way his by merit.

Chapter 19 - Sir Geoffrey Stanning. Father of Five

Sir Geoffrey left his meeting with Sir Crispin Jessop deep in thought. He had always tried to erase Nicola and more importantly, their child from his mind. "She'd be fine," he had told himself over and over again. He had his own family to concentrate on. The children were fine, healthy kids who looked very photogenic alongside his wife in the many family pictures the press had published over the years. Their futures were far more important to him than the result of any wild seeds sown in his youth; not that he had exactly been a youth when he was first elected, but the principle was the same.

On this occasion, though, he couldn't dismiss thoughts of his daughter so easily. What had happened to her? Had she survived the early death of her mother? He didn't want to start hunting for her but he would dearly love the reassurance of knowing that she had grown up happy and healthy. All he knew about her really was that her birthday had been almost exactly nine months after his election to Parliament for the first time. That would have made it sometime early in February. No he thought, he could work out exactly when it was. He had last spoken to Nicola the day before the then Prime Minister survived a vote of confidence on Europe. There had been a big reshuffle and Geoffrey became PPS to the Minister for Rural affairs as a thank you for his loyalty. Nicola had said their child had been born three days before they spoke.

Back at his office he looked back first at his diaries which he always kept and then at the calendar on his computer until he found the relevant year and worked it out. She must have been born on 10th February, 29 years previously. Almost 30 years ago, as it was the 7th of February that day. In three days time his daughter would be 30 years of age, assuming she had survived everything that life had thrown at her along the way. All the things he had been unable to help her with or prepare her for. Two years older than his oldest son with Marilyn. His mind roamed over all the possibilities, both likely and fanciful. What if she was destitute and needed his help. What if she was now comfortably off and tried to find him. What if one of his sons and daughter met? What if... what if... what if?

He was rudely disturbed from his daydreaming by a call from the PM who wanted to discuss the current security state and, no doubt arrange another COBRA meeting, largely so he could tell the press he had called another COBRA meeting. For the present Sir Geoffrey had to put all thoughts of his daughter from his mind and answer the call to duty. But only for the present.

The following few days saw a flurry of activity around the Prime Minister which kept Sir Geoffrey far busier than he would have liked. He was constantly on the phone to officials or the press as well as co-ordinating the off the record briefings to the media in the background. The days were long and at the end of them he was so tired that he collapsed into the bed in his room at Dudley's and fell asleep as soon as his head hit the pillow.

He was in the middle of the maelstrom when he noticed an otherwise trivial email from Brian Smithe, the poor bugger pitted against the Harpie across the dispatch box. It was an invitation to casual drinks for the birthday of his junior researcher, Susan White. Sir Geoffrey would have skimmed past it normally were it not for the date. It was that evening and the date was the 10th of February. She was going to be 30. Brian was inviting anybody who could make it at short notice.

Sir Geoffrey sat back in his chair, ignoring the carnage of urgent things to do on his desk. He could only vaguely picture Brian's researcher and could not have told you her name. Now though, he trawled his memory for any trace of what she looked like. She had been born on the 10th February, 30 years before. It was too much of a coincidence that she had ended up in an office here in Westminster, working for a party colleague. There must have been thousands of girls born on that day. There was no way, surely, that she was his daughter.

Ignoring everything that he had planned to do that evening, he replied that he would be delighted to attend, albeit briefly due to the pressures of work at this time. As soon as he sent the email he wished he hadn't but he was a man of his word and would have to go. The unlikelihood of this being Nicola's daughter, his daughter, was such that his actions surprised himself, though not quite as much as they surprised Brian Smithe when he realised that the Prime Minister's PPS was making the effort to attend the birthday bash for his junior researcher.

The day dragged on for a change but eventually it came to the time that Sir Geoffrey could arrive at Susan White's birthday celebration without it looking as if he particularly wanted to. On arrival he was reminded why he would not normally attend such events. Brian Smithe was there with a few other MPs but no other cabinet members or anyone of note. A few other researchers were there as were a few wives and/or girlfriends but overall the turnout was poor. Sir Geoffrey picked out Susan immediately by virtue of a large '30 today' badge pinned to her lapel. She was standing beside Brian; a little too closely perhaps for Geoffrey's liking but it was all in-house so nobody else noticed or cared. He walked towards her, taking in every aspect of her looks as he did so. She was pretty and reminded him vaguely of his paternal Aunt Beatrice. This likeness did not prove or disprove anything but he could hear his grandmother's voice saying 'blood will out' as he approached.

Brian looked round with a mixture of pride and panic as Sir Geoffrey arrived.

"Thank you for coming Sir Geoffrey. I appreciate you taking the time. This is Susan; the birthday girl."

Sir Geoffrey stared intensely into Susan's face as he shook her hand, wished her a happy birthday and handed over the box of hand-made chocolates his secretary had purchased earlier that day.

"Not at all," said Sir Geoffrey. "I am always keen to meet the team behind each minister and this is an ideal opportunity. It's also nice to get away from the office at the moment, even for a short time."

He took a glass of white bubbly wine that was offered and knew it was not champagne from the first sip. It wasn't even a decent substitute but he certainly wasn't there for the free drinks. Instead he managed to engage Susan in small talk about current events in and out with

Parliament with an intensity which convinced her that he was trying to chat her up.

Instead Sir Geoffrey was looking for any hint of Nicola in her expressions. Her hair was of a similar colour and she was about the same height. When she laughed which was not as often or as easily as Nicola had done there was a slight resemblance to the carefree manner he had failed to completely erase from his mind. Could she be their daughter? He wasn't sure. These passing similarities to Nicola were nowhere near enough to convince him. The vision of his Aunt Beatrice kept returning to his mind, though, so he could not completely rule it out.

After a longer time than Brian had expected, Sir Geoffrey made his excuses and left, allowing most of the people in the room to breathe easily again and for Sue to tuck into the Cava before eventually heading home for a romp with the Minister for Families.

After Susan's birthday bash Sir Geoffrey was unsettled in a way which he had managed to avoid most of his adult life. Phlegmatic didn't begin to describe his usual persona and in fairness he maintained a public face of calmness and unflappability, seeing it as necessary to reassure the public, should they need it. Underneath the surface, though, a stream of unanswered questions formed a constant distraction to his concentration. It was a hundred to one shot that Susan was actually his daughter though everything seemed to add up, even the ghost of dear old Aunt Beatrice. Beyond that Sue seemed to highlight the fact that somewhere, out there, was a daughter he had never met and never asked about.

Sir Geoffrey found himself at work or occasionally at family events lost in a world of speculation. His attention span was poor and his usual focus on events deserted him at times to the point that even the Prime Minister commented. Not to Sir Geoffrey's face of course, but as usual via the chief whip. Sir Crispin waited for a suitable moment and took his colleague aside in Dudley's one evening after a private dinner with the PM and just a few major donors who had essentially paid for the privilege of a private event to lobby in a forum not available to anyone else, least of all the electorate.

"You seem a bit pre-occupied these days, old boy," began Sir Crispin in a manner Sir Geoffrey immediately recognised as indicating the PM's concern.

"I'm not sleeping well, that's all," said Sir Geoffrey trying to fob off his colleague and avoid any lengthy conversation. He had no intention of discussing anything of what was preying on his mind and he knew he would not be expected to. It was a game really. The bottom line was a message; Pull your socks up; we're worried about your performance.

Without revealing anything of his inner conflict, Sir Geoffrey got a grip of himself and during the rest of the exchange sniped back sufficiently at Sir Crispin to reassure him that he was still on top of things and could handle his end of the PM's duties.

After that uncomfortable encounter he managed to focus again on his daily routine and dismiss all thoughts of his daughter with Nicola from his mind. Well, almost all thoughts. He knew the dangers he would face if Sir Crispin smelled blood and he raised his game enough to prevent any further action there. He found himself, however, looking at women of Susan's age in a different way as he walked through parliament or was driven through London. Where was she? Was she okay? Did she ever wonder about her father, or had Nicola provided a cover story for her relatives? Was it really Susan White?

Whatever else he might have been thinking about in the background he was now firmly focused again on his day job. The Prime Minister was concerned about a number of things. He was mainly concerned about winning the next election and ensuring a second term in office for himself. That meant that he was very concerned about everything which threatened that possibility. His concern at the moment was particularly focussed on a number of poor performances by ministers in his cabinet. Partly this was due to the fact that some were there for reasons of unswerving loyalty rather than ability. In other cases though, the opposition had managed to attract very good people. Couple this with a few of his cabinet disagreeing with some of the recent legislation he had introduced and it all spelt trouble. They did not disagree with him openly at cabinet meetings but it was clear that some were unhappy with his changes to benefits, largely as it threatened their majorities or those of their own supporters in Parliament. A few had been briefing behind his back and one had evenly been recorded at a supposedly private constituency meeting calling the bedroom tax 'suicide in the marginals'. When this went viral the minister concerned, Brian Smithe, had publically backtracked enough to save his political skin but it had resonated with the voters and emboldened some of the PM's more serious rivals. Sir Geoffrey would have advised the PM to sack Brian Smithe immediately for disloyalty had it not been for the fact that his opposite number, Dawn Harper, had been completely outclassing Brian in debate after debate. To sack the Minister for Families for any reason now could be interpreted as a scalp for the opposition. The mouthy political correspondent on Channel Four news had already hinted at this in a report about one of The Harpie's recent performances. The last thing the PM needed was him saying I told you so as a minister was sacked.

Sir Geoffrey had to play this one correctly. The Prime Minister was relying on his knowledge and experience. For the moment then he had to put any thoughts of his daughter to the side and concentrate on the demise of Dawn Harper. At the very least he had to come up with a way of shutting up Brian Smithe or getting rid of him without it being seen as a victory for the opposition. The government had enough to deal with without somebody of Dawn's ability moving up the ranks of power against them.

Chapter 20 - Watch with Mother

As the domestic arrangements in the safe house settled into as close a thing to a routine as could be managed, the troops regularly found themselves with little to do. After working out, checking weapons and the usual personal admin required each day there was little left to do except, read, sleep or watch television.

The television was of no use in terms of distracting the twins at their early age but it was a useful distraction for the adults in the house. Sue would regularly find herself watching daytime or night-time TV with two or three of her house mates who all tried and failed to curb their language on such occasions. All except Mac whose language never varied from the profane. A casual observer meeting him for the first time would have been forgiven for assuming he had Tourettes Syndrome.

Sue didn't really mind the bad language, she was used to far worse from MPs and at least the soldiers insulted each other directly to the face rather than behind each other's backs as was normal in the world of politics. In fact it would be fair to say that she looked forward to watching television with them, especially when as many as possible would crowd together in the lounge and watch the news. It was partly a diversion from the boredom but it was also to try and gauge what was happening elsewhere and to figure out when they would be called upon to act or be sent back to Hereford and stood down.

It became clear to them at these times that trying to gauge anything from the interviews with politicians was pointless. They knew they would hear soon enough if they were needed and long before it made the news but there was a feeling amongst some that there could be a hint dropped somewhere or another.

Sue tried to translate some of the language used based on her experience of working with Brian and his department and soon found her own vocabulary descended to the gutter when explaining what some of the figures were actually saying. This endeared her to all of the troops beyond the usual level of being the only woman in a house full of men locked away from the world.

"He's a wanker," was Mac's considered opinion of the Prime Minister each time he appeared.

One time the PM was pushed on whether or not he had authorised the SAS to operate in London during the current security alert.

"We're famous," shouted Sandy Shaw from the couch and the others joined in, offering autographs and quoting their fees for interviews.

Mac shushed them and they stopped to listen to what the PM was saying.

"I can confirm only that this government will not rule out any legal options in the fight against terrorists and that would obviously include the armed services if appropriate and requested by the police through the Home Secretary."

The interviewer followed up the previous question he had asked.

"There have been unconfirmed reports that a new SAS unit, nicknamed Blue Thunder and consisting of 70 specially trained troops who are on permanent standby to fly anywhere in the country, has been created. Can you confirm that Prime Minister?"

The Prime Minister looked at the camera in a theatrical way as if he would like to give more details before simply adding: "The government never comments on the activities of our Special Forces."

There was a cheer in the front room before Ray shushed them again.

"Shut the fuck up. You'll wake the kids."

Sue loved it and even found that she was no longer scared of either Mac or John the Beast. She had discovered that the latter was the most well read of the group and could quote everything from Shakespeare to Tolstoy. She discovered none of this from John himself as he spoke rarely but pieced it together from admiring comments the others made about him. Although he had admitted early on that he had no children, he had proved adept at changing nappies, burping the tiny tots on his massive shoulders or feeding them gently with a plastic spoon which was largely hidden in his hands. The twins had initially appeared traumatised by the scary man holding a jar of food but the quickest way to a baby's heart is through its stomach and they soon took his bulky frame in their stride. For some reason they seemed to adore Mac. Nobody understood that one beyond the fact that he and his wife had four children somewhere in darkest Glasgow.

Chapter 21 – Jack Hunter

Jack Hunter had been the school bully at both his Primary school and at his comprehensive school thereafter. He was big from an early age and grew to be six foot three and fourteen stone in weight by the age of fifteen. As a result he was free to roam the school playground during his school days and pick on the smaller boys, which was most of them, either for profit or pleasure. He was as happy stealing dinner money from them as he was frightening them for the sake of it. By the time he left high school even most of the teachers were scared of him. He started various dead-end jobs over the next three years before deciding that his future lay with the local police force. The realisation came to him one day while he was a passenger in a works van which had been stopped for speeding. The driver was in his forties and had worked for the firm of freight forwarders for years. He put on the air of an old sweat who could take care of himself in any situation but Jack had been impressed at how quickly the sight of police uniforms had made him both nervous and polite. Here was the job for Jack.

Having avoided any serious trouble and being fairly fit, Jack had seemed the ideal candidate to join the Met when he applied and as a result he soon found himself carrying out his basic training as a police cadet. He had to bite his tongue a couple of times during the weeks of drill and instruction but managed to do so and graduate as a rooky policeman. As was usual at that time he was put on the beat with an experience police constable of fifteen years' service who had indeed seen most things in his time. The theory went that young police officers would learn the ropes from a more experienced colleague and thus become better policemen. The reality was instead that they quickly learned the short cuts and bad habits inherent within the force and readily adopted the canteen culture and prejudices of their senior mentors. To do otherwise would have made it very difficult to continue. Most recruits with strong principles and an aversion to lying under oath to support a colleague soon fell by the wayside. Jack Hunter, however, lapped it up.

Jack immediately felt at home in a job where he was soon able to abuse his power and to assault suspects on a regular basis with impunity. By reputation he was soon known as the kind of guy to have beside you in a fight and was seconded for many raids on criminals of all kinds, often as the first man through the newly broken down door. After several years of uniformed service his exploits brought him to the attention of the flying squad who liked his approach and he was transferred, finding himself regularly involved in the arrest of aggressive professional criminals. The icing on the cake came when he was selected for firearms training and thereafter allowed to walk the streets, or at least drive them on occasions, tooled up. He became a very good shot, fired several shots in anger on one raid and even acquired his very own revolver after finding it hidden in a villains lock-up. All in all, life was good.

This idyllic set up lasted for 18 years with Jack making sergeant along the way and would have continued until retirement were it not for the unfortunate death in custody of a black drugs dealer. Cause of death was inconclusive but a major factor was a severe beating which the suspect had sustained at some stage between the time of his arrest and the time of death ten hours later. As arresting officer, Jack had to carry the can. On reflection this was only fair, as he had been the person holding the arms of the deceased during the beating.

He was put on leave pending investigation and stayed at home expecting the hammer to fall at any time. He was interviewed under oath as were the other two officers present at the time and a file was prepared. The process dragged on as such things do and the press was briefly involved in a lukewarm campaign by a local community leader to bring the guilty to justice. The dead man had few friends outwith his immediate family, which consisted largely of his sister. He was well known as a bad man in his neighbourhood and most people who had known him considered his death to be just desserts, irrespective of how it may have occurred. The evidence mounted up though and a new Commissioner had risen to the post on the back of a promise to change the culture within the Metropolitan police so something had to be done and done publicly. How publicly could be massaged behind the scenes, but a police officer would have to be at least sacked to show the Commissioner's commitment to keeping his word.

The hammer was prepared as the two more junior officers were cleared of any guilt and Jack realised he was for the chop. What he didn't know, however, was the fact that the coroner had been impressed with Jack's style and had mentioned as much at lunch in Dudley's one day. Discreet enquiries were made thereafter and Jack was identified as a possible person of use.

Chapter 22 – Jack gets a new job

Two days after his junior colleagues had been cleared of serious wrongdoing, Jack received a call ordering him to attend a disciplinary meeting at nine o'clock the following morning. He put the phone down and looked at the clock. It was two thirty in the afternoon. That gave him enough time to drink himself stupid and sober up enough to face the music, but only just. He set the alarm on his phone for seven a.m.

He opened a new bottle of whisky and poured himself the first of many generous measures. The alcohol started to work its magic in his body and the reality of his predicament began to ease slightly. By the fourth glass he was no longer overly concerned. It was the end of his police career, the end of his pension and might even involve a court case and jail. Not great news he thought but he had had a good run. By the time the bottle was finished he couldn't care less, nor could he stay conscious.

As he had expected, Jack woke the next day with a blinding headache and a severe hangover. It took him a few minutes to focus on the alarm and work out how to stop the noise it was making. He then took a further moment or two to remember why he had got drunk and exactly how much shit he was in. As planned, this was the low moment of his day, whatever happened thereafter. The realisation and the hangover combined made him feel dreadful. Irrespective of what the disciplinary meeting involved he would slowly but surely start to feel better as the day wore on. A drastic approach perhaps; but one which had worked for him before. For now though, he felt and smelt terrible. Time for a shower.

Once clean he made himself a strong mug of coffee and waited for the stimulus of the caffeine. As it kicked in he started to feel slightly better. Then he threw up and made another mug, this time without his customary two sugars. He kept it down and had another quick shower to wash off the sweat from the vomiting and the hangover. Then he dressed in the suit and tie he kept ready for funerals. It was his newest and smartest, being needed occasionally but not worn regularly for work. He looked in the mirror. He looked smartly dressed but his skin was ashen in colour.

The next part of his plan involved walking a mile and a half at speed to the tube station which would take him directly to the building where the hearing was to be held. He could have taken one closer and changed but he badly needed the fresh air, not wanting to show up looking grey and scared. He covered the distance quickly, bought a bacon sandwich with far too much brown sauce on it and ate it on the tube. By the time it arrived at his stop he was starting to feel far better than when he had awoken. Not yet good, but better. This realisation made the hearing merely a part of the day's road to recovery.

He arrived in time to have a pee in the gents, straighten his tie and hair then walk to the designated briefing room five minutes early. A uniformed constable was posted outside the door and nodded at Jack as he arrived.

"You're to take a seat for now, Sir," he said. "They are in deep discussion at the moment and will call you in when they're ready."

Jack nodded and gratefully sat down outside the room. He was actually feeling quite good now as the exercise and the unsubtle combination of salts and sauces brought his body back towards normal. His plan had worked. Instead of waking and dreading the meeting he had woken and been distracted by the hangover. Now that he was outside and about to hear his sorry fate, he was feeling better by the minute.

The door of the room opened and a uniformed inspector stuck his head out.

"Right Sergeant Hunter, the disciplinary panel are ready for you," he said formally and held the door open for Jack to walk through.

Inside, behind a long table, sat three men and a woman, with a further chair at the end which the uniformed Inspector re-occupied. The other figures were a lawyer acting for the Met (Jack had waived his right to any representation early on, seeing the defence of his actions as pointless), a representative from the Police Federation, a civilian employee taking notes and the chairman of the panel, Deputy Assistant Commissioner Gordon.

Jack sat on the seat facing the panel and waited to learn his fate. Before that, however, he learned many other things from DAC Gordon. He learned that there was a cancer in the heart of The Met. Jack learned that he himself was part of that disease and that Gordon was determined to cut it out for the benefit of the general health of the force. Jack also learned, through another metaphor, that he was a dinosaur, a violent beast whose time had come and who had become extinct. Presumably, Gordon was a Jurassic hunter who had been sent to put down dinosaurs along with being a skilled surgeon. Jack briefly thought the Met might be reduced to a level barely large enough to field a football team if Gordon continued unchecked but he knew he had been caught in the act and they had to make an example of him. This was not the start of any clear-out. Finally Jack learned what he had secretly already known; that he was no longer a policeman, that he had no pension to look forward to and that future references from The Met would say ‘dismissed for gross misconduct’.

He was asked if he had anything to say. Whilst drunk he had thought up a load of cocky answers to that one, most of which he had since forgotten. He briefly considered tell the DAC to go and fuck himself but didn’t have the energy anymore. He opted for the traditional stoic approach of "don’t explain, don’t complain".

“No, Sir,” was all he said.

“Inspector Johnston here will take your badge and complete the formalities,” DAC Gordon informed him before closing his file, handing it to Johnston and leaving with the rest of the panel in tow.

When the panel had left and were safely out of earshot, Inspector Johnston mellowed slightly.

“Sorry about this Jack, but I’ll need your badge and all your keys. Then I have to escort you to your desk where you will have 30 minutes to collect any personal items. Then I’ll walk you to the door. Paperwork confirming the panel's decision and any appeals procedure will be sent this week along with details of your final pay.”

Jack nodded and handed over his warrant card and security pass along with various keys to his locker, filing cabinets and the door of his office. The ‘formalities’ were gone through exactly as Johnston had outlined them and Jack found himself outside the Headquarters building a mere 46 minutes after the panel had handed down their judgement.

"Now what?" thought Jack to himself. "Still, at least the hangover has gone."

The short term plan was easy. He headed for a bar where he knew some of his former colleagues were waiting to hear his fate. Getting pissed with them would sort out the rest of the day. After that, the future would take care of itself, he hoped.

Chapter 23 - Jack Hunter 2

While Jack was heading for the bar to meet up with the rest of his squad a strange thing was happening to the file of case notes which had been passed to Inspector Johnston. He had headed for his office to complete the checklist of actions before taking it to DAC Gordon for final approval and administration. As he was working on it there was a knock on his door and two men in suits walked into his office. One of them showed a warrant card indicating that he was from Special Branch. A brief discussion followed during which Johnston was informed that Special Branch had an interest in the case which had implications for National Security, and that they required the file along with any other paperwork which he held about Jack Hunter. Johnston was at first reluctant but when his phone went and DAC Gordon authorised the request he handed the file over along with his own briefing notes for the panel. The men left quickly without any pleasantries and Johnston sat there bemused.

"What on earth has Hunter beating up a drug supplier got to do with National Security?"

After a moment's pause though, he returned to his own in tray, aware that questioning the actions of Special Branch would be unwise.

Chapter 24 - A New Beginning For Hunter

The following day Jack woke with what he was relieved to find was only a minor hangover. The events of the previous day flowed back into his consciousness and he groaned, then turned over in bed. Strangely enough he managed to get back to sleep but was awoken at nine o'clock exactly by his doorbell.

"Piss off," he hissed and turned over again.

The doorbell rang again, this time for a long time and he realised whoever it was was not going away. He stood up and wrapped an old and rather threadbare dressing gown round his frame, having found himself to be wearing only a pair of Y-fronts.

He opened the door and found a large man in a very smart suit standing there holding a thin valise.

"Jack Hunter?" he asked in a way that suggested he already knew it was.

"Who wants to know?" asked Jack, angry at being woken up and being at a disadvantage in dress state to a complete stranger.

"The name's Smith, Special Branch," said the man flashing an ID card slightly too quickly for Jack to focus on it. With surprising agility he sidestepped Hunter and walked into the flat.

"Hey, I didn't say you could come in," shouted Jack as the man headed into the living room of the flat.

"That's not very welcoming, Jack," said the man who claimed to be called Smith.

"You're not very welcome, and I'm not in the mood for company. You can fuck off out of my house, whoever you are and whoever you work for."

"I may be the only friend you have in the world at this moment in time so don't be so hasty," said Smith.

Jack was about to answer back when he suddenly realised the possible truth of the man's statement. He had never made friends easily and didn't expect many of his former colleagues in the flying squad to keep in touch now. The farewell at the pub had been lively but had a feeling of obligatory attendance about it, as if it could have been any one of those present who had been sacked for such an offence. Now that he was a civilian who had left the squad in disgrace it would be bad news for any of them to be seen associating with him on a regular, social basis. All in all it wouldn't take long to clear the Christmas cards from his mantelpiece next year.

"How exactly are you my friend? In case you hadn't heard I was banned from the force yesterday in unfavourable circumstances. I'm an ex-copper with no job prospects beyond security at the local supermarket, and even that might be beyond my reach if they ask for detailed references."

"You haven't been banned yet," said Smith to Hunter's surprise.

"Really? I had to turn in my warrant card, keys, even my fucking handcuffs yesterday before being escorted from the premises. By now the paperwork will be signed, sealed and delivered to personnel who will be writing to me shortly with my fuck-off papers."

"No they won't," said Smith.

"What makes you so sure?" asked Jack.

"Because I have all the papers here and they haven't been signed yet by the Chairman of your Disciplinary Panel, DAC Gordon. Nor will they if you come and work for me."

Smith had opened the valise as he spoke and, taking out the forms which Jack had signed the day before with Inspector Johnston handed them over for verification.

"How… I don't understand," stammered Jack.

"Will you come and work for me? If you do, all this paperwork will disappear and you will continue to be paid as a Detective Sergeant exactly as before."

"Transfer to Special Branch?" asked Jack. "I wouldn't have a clue where to begin with protection and the like. I've concentrated on making sure people came to harm recently in case you hadn't noticed."

"That is what we would want you to continue doing and it wouldn't exactly be Special Branch per se. You would be based at home and be freelance, carrying out special jobs as required."

"This sounds a bit dodgy to me. How do I know I can trust you?"

"You don't; but then you don't have many options. In here is a genuine warrant card, identifying you as a sergeant in Special Branch, and a gun. If you agree to this offer you get both and keep getting paid, including your full pension entitlement. If you don't, then good luck with your new career stopping local shoplifters."

Jack stared at Smith to gauge how serious he was and found his gaze returned from pitiless black eyes. Whoever this guy was he meant business. Jack doubted he could throw him out of the flat if he wanted to and wasn't sure this was an offer he could refuse. All in all it looked like the best option he had at the moment, although he doubted Smith would ever become a friend.

"Supposing I said yes, what sort of work would this involve?" asked Jack indicating he was amenable to giving the offer serious consideration.

"From time to time you would be asked to speak to people and persuade them either to refrain from certain actions or to make sure they carried out certain actions, some of which may appear to contravene the law. You will of course have the full protection of Special Branch in all your actions. Providing you carry out the tasks to the letter without question you will effectively be immune from prosecution."

"What if I showed up at Special Branch Head Office and said hello, can I come to the Christmas Party?" asked Jack.

"That would be very unwise," said Smith. "You are not on the books, as it were, as far as mainstream staff are concerned. You work for me and answer to me. All instructions come from me and you only ever work with somebody else if I say so. Stick to that and I guarantee you will have a long and fruitful career."

"And if I don't?"

,"This file can be actioned at any point if necessary, though other sanctions are possible. In case you are still swithering I have here a payslip with your gratuity lump sum included along with a full and final month's pay as a Metropolitan police sergeant. It reflects 18 years of unblemished service. Agree to work for me now and that amount goes into your account this Friday. Then you continue to be paid as a sergeant, including all the increments."

"I assume if I don't agree that paperwork gets actioned immediately."

"You catch on fast, Jack. The choice is yours of course."

"How could I refuse; where do I sign?"

"I don't think a signature is either necessary or wise. We shake hands and you are onboard."

Jack shook hands with Smith who then handed over a warrant card, the payslip and a standard issue 9mm pistol.

"No handcuffs?" quipped Jack.

“Your days of taking people into custody before beating them up are over, Jack,” said Smith with a look that suggested he was deadly serious.

“Now what do I do?” asked Jack.

“You wait. When we need you I will phone you. Stay available, stay fairly sober and stay out of trouble.”

With that, Smith left.

Jack sat down on his sofa and tried to make sense of what had just happened. He appeared to be employed again, all of a sudden, and with money about to arrive in his bank account. He was armed and could identify himself as a policeman if needs be. He looked again at the warrant card which seemed genuine enough. The payslip too was impressive. When he looked carefully at the pistol though he noticed something he had missed before. The serial number had been filed off. An uneasy feeling spread through him as if he had just sold his soul to the devil.

"That was okay, though," he thought to himself. "I’m a pretty evil son of a bitch myself."

Chapter 25 - A Rival to the Throne

James Jessop was the nephew of Sir Crispin Jessop the Chief Whip. At first sight the two could almost have been father and son. Rumours might have started had it not been public knowledge that Sir Crispin was a life-long bachelor with no interest in the opposite sex. They were however close in many ways and young James had chosen to follow his uncle into politics rather than merchant banking, where his father had made his mark. With the family wealth he had behind him James would find it easy to succeed in any field of endeavour, but with Sir Crispin's support too he had not only found himself a safe seat at an early age but had also risen through the ranks to become a junior minister by the age of 32. He took on the Transport brief following a reshuffle when he was 35, with considerable success as far as the party faithful were concerned. He had managed to privatise many aspects of the railway network deemed unprofitable and successfully disguised the subsidies required to do so. He had sold off great swathes of land previously owned by what had been British Rail and farmed out contracts for motorway maintenance left right and centre. In short he was seen by many as a future leader who would ensure a favourable return on any capital invested in his rise to the Prime Minister's job.

For his part, James was focused on nothing else. He had an intense dislike for the Pearson dynasty for no other reason than that he felt that they should be replaced by the older and more established Jessop dynasty who, after all, had been sending their children to Eton for seven generations now, not just two. His father's work in the city held no interest for him; he would get that money in due course. After all, the family owned most of Barton and Jessops between them. Instead he was drawn to the wielding of true power which he had sensed his uncle possessed in a way his father never would. There was of course a cross over between the two. You didn't get far in politics without money behind you. And, as many found out, you got nowhere with money dead set against you.

James was five years younger than Charles Pearson the Prime Minister and their paths had hardly crossed at school. Sir Henry Pearson and Sir Crispin Jessop however, had almost been contemporaries, Henry being one year older than Crispin. James Jessop had always sensed an ancient enmity between his uncle and the Prime Minister's father but nothing specific had ever been expressed in conversation. Instead Sir Crispin had immediately thrown his weight behind young James when he expressed an interest in politics and quickly saw his rise as a contest between the families.

James loved politics from the outset and felt at home as soon as he walked into the Palace of Westminster, initially as an intern for one of Sir Crispin's colleagues but soon thereafter as a Member of Parliament in his own right. He had no nerves when making his maiden speech and found that many of the other MPs were people he knew or knew of from his family's circle of friends. It was more like joining a club than starting a career, although he took the job of progressing within it very seriously.

In this respect his uncle was an invaluable ally. His experience of Parliament and its ways, coupled with a complete lack of either conscience or loyalty to anybody outwith the immediate family circle, made him very effective and, as James quickly learned, a formidable foe. Anyone who stood in the way of James' advancement soon found themselves the target for Sir Crispin's political skills. Most were completely oblivious to the dangers until it was too late. He had the ability to appear friendly and innocuous to everyone in the rank and file while also seeming, correctly, indispensible to the senior members of the party. As a result he occupied a position of respect and fear within the party. Anyone with a problem of any kind knew that Sir Crispin was the man to sort it for them but they also knew that his help came at a price.

For their part, the Pearsons had achieved success within parliament without feeling overly indebted to Sir Crispin or any other member of the Jessop clan. They were very wealthy due largely to the efforts of Sir Henry Pearson's father George, who had lived a rags-to-riches life by marrying into a family of arms manufacturers at the outset of World War One. By the end of the war his in-laws were retired from the business or had been killed in the war and he was not only running the business but owned most of it through some fast footwork round his new wife and her few remaining family members.

He invested heavily in his son's education and war-related industries, becoming a friend of Sir Winston Churchill in time to profit from preparations for the Second World War. 'Winnie' as he called the future Prime Minister , visited the family's estate in Norfolk and sought advice and support from, by that time, Sir George, on the preparation for 'the coming storm'. Sir George was well positioned to profit from the provision of all material needed for war and had sole rights to raw materials from some parts of the empire. He was a safe pair of hands as far as Churchill was concerned when it came to making use of these resources, and if he profited personally from it then that was only right and proper.

The Second World War proved to be even more profitable for the family than the first had been. Sir George was too old and valuable to the war effort to serve and young Henry was a schoolboy, meaning the war left them untouched as a family as far as loss and suffering went. They lost the butler from the town house, which was itself only slightly damaged by the bombs and two junior servants from the country estate in Norfolk. Fortunately their country butler had served in the First World War, and a gassing at Mons meant he was ineligible for further military service. The fresh Norfolk air kept him in relatively good health at least.

Using his wealth and contacts Sir George easily secured a place at Eton for young Henry, against Winnie's advice to send him to Harrow. After the war, George realised Churchill was a spent force and the family needed a wider circle of contacts to cement their position. He also wanted Henry to go into politics and gain real power and influence; that would be best for the family's business interests. Henry went to Eton where he found some reluctant to accept him, being the first of his family to go there. In his turn he found himself backed by his father and his wealth to an extent that even established families couldn't match. All this helped him be elected to Pop and to end his time at Eton with a range of contacts which would be the envy of anybody entering any field, be it politics, business or academia. If any of the fellows there objected to his popularity or his family's recent financial success, as some like the Jessops did, he had the backing to bait them mercilessly with relative impunity.

When Henry left Eton he went to Oxford, eventually achieving a third in Philosophy, Politics and Economics. Most of his time there though was spent in the company of the offspring of some of the wealthiest families in the country. They had a reputation for partying and wild living that scandalised those who were easily scandalised and made them the envy of those who could not participate. It was a very exclusive group. If you had to ask the price of anything, ever, then you were not welcome. Sir George found himself paying out constantly for everything from bar bills, food, drink and lodgings to tailor's bills and bail. Some fathers might have objected to these excesses but Sir George saw every penny as an investment in his family's future as part of the ruling elite. If Henry didn't make it to the very top of society then he was establishing himself with the people who might ensure that the next generation of Pearson's did. It was all, therefore, money well spent.

Henry entered politics in due course and rose within the Conservative Party. Although he knew everyone who was anyone in either party he lacked the true ambition to make it all the way to the top job. He married well, to another titled family of long pedigree who weren't too much of a drain on the Pearson's resources and they produced three healthy children, one of whom, Charles, showed promise from the outset. Sir George lived long enough to see his grandson start Eton and show the promise of a bright future. Grandfather would take long walks with grandson during which a vision of a family destiny would be outlined, discussed and eventually shared. By the time Sir George died his son and grandson saw it is a natural course of events that young Charles should be Prime Minister, via Eton, Oxford and a safe seat procured by family connections. And so it transpired with an almost effortless sequence of planned events. Within that journey the Pearsons, father and son, rather took for granted the help provided by the Jessop family bank and Sir Crispin Jessop in particular. A few words of thanks along the way might have helped soothe the ire of Sir Crispin, but it might not have. Some slights suffered in his younger days at school were not so easily forgiven or forgotten.

Chapter 26 - Matinee Idol

The safe house settled into a routine after a while and Susan noticed that the man referred to as 'Boss' was away most of the time. She had noticed Jason immediately her initial terror abated when the troops arrived at first. He was in his early thirties as far as she could tell but had the look of somebody who had seen and lived a lot in the years he had had. He was about six feet tall and had a very fit but not overly muscled build. His face was a chiselled, leading man sort and the overall impression was of an alpha male amongst alpha males. He was the Milk Tray man she had dreamed of breaking into her house with a box of chocolates but also choosing to stay the night, now come to life and become James Bond for real into the bargain. She found herself attracted to him as any woman would have been, but didn't fancy her chances of him feeling anything for her. He made Brian Smithe seem dull as dishwater. Even the name Jason seemed to fit with his persona perfectly; if not a Greek God then at least a classical hero of the first order.

He came to the house on a regular basis with or without the oldest of the group, Old Bob and immediately commanded the attention of the others. He brought little in the way of news as far as she could tell as she was not included in the briefings. The others kept her abreast of things though. Mac was often the best one to get a summary from.

"Anything new?" she would ask him after Jason had left each time.

"Fuck all," was Mac's usual reply.

Occasionally it would be expanded to, "Load of bollocks," or "Chinese bloody whispers."

It was only towards the end of her time with the guys that Mac admitted, "Something's about to happen, maybe." He was very quickly proved right.

Jason didn't exactly ignore Susan. He would ask if she was okay and if the guys were looking after her and the twins. He seemed to genuinely care but she suspected that it was based more on avoiding problems or a complaint later than caring for her specifically. Even so, she liked the concern when he showed it. On a few occasions he would make a cup of tea or coffee for both of them and sit with her in the front room and make small talk. She would reassure him that the lads were being perfect gentlemen and would joke that they would make a great team for a nursery school if the soldiering thing didn't work out. He would smile politely at her jokes, showing wrinkles on his face that came from the exertion and strain of his job. There was always tension there being his deep brown eyes and she felt instinctively drawn to him. Brian was forgotten completely when she spoke to Jason; there was no comparison as far as she was concerned and she wondered what she had ever seen in him when there men like Jason around.

In a quiet moment one day watching Jeremy Vine with Disco Bob she found herself asking him if Jason was married, before she could stop herself.

Disco Bob looked at her realising she was a little bit smitten with his boss.

"He was once but it didn't last. We're away so much it never lasts. Most of us have a string of failed marriages and relationships behind us: comes with the job. Oh, except Mac who's been married happily for twelve years and has four kids.

"Really," asked Susan surprised. "What's his secret?"

"He's almost never home," said Bob without a hint of humour in his voice, before adding with a smile. "In fact he may only have been home four times since he got married. John the Beast's never been married, saves any hassle."

In a separate but similar conversation with Mac the following day while changing nappies, she managed to bring the conversation round to the same topic to see if Jason had anyone special in his life. The answer wasn't either of the ones she had expected or one she wanted.

"No, he shags for Britain and moves on. Best way really."

"Thank you for your usual tact and honesty," she thought to herself, but it was a warning in a way. "How can that be the best way?"

"Simple," said Mac. "This is a high risk occupation. We don't get to go home very often. Not everyone gets to go home at all. Easiest way is not to get involved too seriously with women. The Boss learned that the hard way."

"What about you though? You're happily married aren't you? What does your wife think about you being away all the time?"

"She loves it. I just get in the way at home. But that's different."

Mac didn't expand as to why it was different for him and his wife but as he seemed to break all the other rules in life she wasn't surprised and didn't press him further. She had got an insight into Jason and that was progress enough.

Jason Mountford had joined the Parachute Regiment after university, where he had gained a pass degree in Russian and Spanish. During his time as a student, he had joined the Officer Training Corps and quickly realised the army was the way ahead for him. He was already a keen skier and had gained a black belt in Karate at the age of 14. He needed a constant series of challenges to stem the boredom of day to day life and the army offered a constant never ending supply. Basic training, fitness tests, Officer Training, P Company and a then a tour of duty in Iraq led to attempting selection for The SAS. He completed the final test despite breaking his leg half way round but because he was outside the permitted time he failed. Hospital, physio and intensive training followed and he passed second time round. Once through selection, his training started in earnest and he had all the challenges even he could handle. High altitude parachuting, sniper training, diving and explosives; it never seemed to end. By the time his training had actually been completed he was so immersed in the way of life he could not imagine anything else. In fact he probably couldn't have adjusted to anything else. He knew that as an officer at some stage in the future he would have to do at least one tour with his own regiment again in order to get on and up the ranks, and he dreaded the prospect. With a bit of luck though, they would be on an operational tour or a war would start or something to make it bearable. Without a constant adrenaline rush he would fall apart.

He met and thought he had fallen in love with a female officer from the Royal Engineers and after a three month romance they married, much against the advice of both their commanding officers. A further three months of romance, passion, enforced separation and mutual suspicion resulted in a permanent split and subsequent divorce. Neither commanding officer actually said "told you so", as they didn't want to lose good officers, and everyone went forward as if the brief marriage had never really happened.

After that, Jason renewed his commitment to The Regiment and following the divorce, regarded love as a brief interlude between bouts of work. His looks and confidence meant he stood out at any social function and women were readily attracted to him. This suited his purposes and he never wanted for female company when he needed it.

When he was working he was 100% focused on the job in hand. When he was on leave he was 100% focused on having a good time and doing what he wanted to do. For that reason, when he arrived at the safe house and discovered there was a woman roughly his age living there with her twins he didn't see a woman at all, even though Susan was attractive. Instead he just saw a problem to be dealt with in the course of the current operation. If he had said as much to Susan he could have saved her a whole lot of time and speculation, not to mention minor heartache along the way. He didn't though; her thoughts and emotions were "her life, her problem" as far as he was concerned.

Chapter 27 – Jihadi Jock

In a flat on the South side of Glasgow Ahmed Khan sat watching a football match. It was an English Premiership match between Chelsea and Manchester City and he was only mildly interested in who won. His real interest lay in the second televised match that day between Glasgow Rangers and Celtic; an Old Firm game. He was an avid Rangers fan and would have been at the match making use of his Ibrox season ticket if he hadn't been on strict orders from his minders to stay at home. He resented this but also understood that for his cover to remain intact he had to remain indoors for the moment. Apart from anything else he had to make sure that no amateur burglar broke into the flat while he was out and stole the timing devices which he was expected to deliver to the other members of his terrorist cell in London.

He had rather hoped he would have carried out this task by now and be back in time for the Old Firm Match but there had been a delay for some reason. No details had been given but he knew it had something to do with press coverage of the Prime Minister's promise to take all necessary steps to safeguard the public from what the

Intelligence Services described as a real and credible threat of a terrorist attack. The Prime Minister had refused to be drawn on whether this included the deployment of troops and specifically members of The Special Air Service in London, but an anonymous source appeared to be telling the entire British Press, off the record, that the SAS were already deployed and ready to swoop.

The most worrying aspect of the press coverage was the focus on a Scottish-born terrorist nicked named Jihadi Jock by the press. While this could also apply to three other members of his cell he was uncomfortable with the publicity of the Scottish connection. This mattered little while he sat in Glasgow watching television, but when he had to go to London with a bag full of bomb detonators he could do without every copper from the Met finding his accent worrying.

For now, though, he could focus on the football. His handlers in the murky world of international intelligence had assured him that he would be allowed to deliver the devices and leave before any assault on the London safe-house. This had been the pattern in previous operations and he had no reason to believe it would be any different this time round. Mossad had recruited him initially and he had been told his current activities were being sanctioned by both MI5 and the CIA. A successful action against a terrorist cell in the run up to a General Election would reassure the public that the present government had everything under control and that intelligence budgets were justified at their present or perhaps slightly higher levels. The rest of the cell were certainly committed to acts of terror and were determined to create a spectacular attack on London. The fact that they would have struggled to obtain the necessary materials for the attack without assistance from a national security agency was not something the British Public had a right to know.

For their part, his immediate handlers were very unhappy with his recent recalcitrance. They had strong views on the timings of events and had spent a lot of time and money making sure that the cell was isolated enough so that without Khan, they could not operate easily within the UK. He had been unhappy with their decision to delay the operation, but they could not have predicted that he himself would inject a subsequent delay, or that it would be based solely on the date of a key Scottish football fixture. For them it was the last straw, and within a remote bunker in the Middle East it had been decided that Ahmed Khan aka Jihadi Jock, had just made himself surplus to requirements. Even if Glasgow Rangers won, they could no longer take his loyalty on trust.

Chapter 28 - Bert Butterfield Gets Closer

The London-based national had loved the idea of an expose involving a Lord Provost and a transvestite Councillor romping round the council chambers at night. It probably wouldn't make their front page but it would make Bert a week's salary in one day.

The story hit the newsstands the following Sunday, augmented with stock photos of both officials taking office, juxtaposed beside pictures of their late night frolics. One of Bert's pictures was in a small box on the cover with the headline "Call me Sally" beside it and enough information to get most readers turning quickly to page five.

The editor of the Sunday Red-top liked the story and most of how Bert had written it. He authorised the agreed payment and asked Bert to come and collect the cheque in person.

"Great stuff," he said to Bert when he arrived at his office. "We didn't even have to change your copy much. If you can bring me more of the same we can do business together but from here on in make it national politicians or celebrities if you can; Smallsville is fine as a one off but our readers won't stay interested in Downfield for long."

Bert left the editor's office on a high. The story had been his big break but to get his photographs used with much of his original writing was a huge boost. He received another smaller payment the following week when the story was run updated with the resignations of both officials and a report of Tom Maybury's suicide.

Bert didn't miss a second's sleep about the news. He had tasted the big time and wanted more. If that was going to happen though, he knew he needed a regular source of scandal in a city he was unfamiliar with. That would not have been easy if he hadn't been something of a computer nerd as well as a journalist. After some intensive study and a few expensive lessons from a shadowy figure recommended by the Red-top's editor, Bert found that he could successfully tap the calls of a number of private individuals when they used their mobiles.

This ability, along with a similar skill for hacking their emails and computers, allowed him to break one story after another during the next ten years. His nose for a story seemed uncanny to many; unexplainable to others who knew he wasn't using any of the usual private detectives they used themselves for phone hacking.

BB as Bert became known in Fleet Street found himself on the payroll of, first the Sunday tabloid he had sold his first story to, then its sister daily paper, on a salary which would have made his old school chums' eyes water.

He managed to survive a press scandal involving other journalists who were caught paying the same professional hacker to get them stories involving prominent people. He was interviewed by police, under caution and also by a parliamentary select committee, and was able to answer honestly that he did not know the hacker involved, nor had he ever used his services to intercept telephone calls. Further he confirmed that he had never used the services of any other hacker, nor would he dream of doing so. 'Of course not: not when I can do it myself.' Nobody seemed to think of asking him that question.

In between revealing scandals he was left largely alone by his editor who assumed, with good reason, that his star reporter would soon bring in yet another scoop if left to his own devices. It was therefore a bit of a surprise to Bert when he was summoned to his editor's office one Monday morning.

"You working on anything at the moment, Bert?" his boss asked him in a pleasant enough way which suggested he was not in any immediate trouble.

"I am always working on something, John; you know me," Bert lied.

"Our patron has a little request for us. Obviously he is not interfering with my independent editorial control."

They both smiled at the joke.

"He is concerned that the government has been looking bad in the headlines recently and has had more than its fair share of dirty laundry washed in public. They are below in the opinion polls and the next general election is too close for his comfort. He would like us to uncover some dirt on the opposition; to even things up a bit - and your name was mentioned. What do you think?"

Bert liked the independence of going for anyone he wanted in public office, and he had been particularly successful uncovering the embarrassing secrets of members of the governing party during the last three years. In hindsight it had been like shooting fish in barrel at times. He resented being asked to take sides, as it were, but he wasn't convinced the pickings would be as rich amongst the members of the shadow cabinet.

"In particular he is concerned at the effectiveness of Dawn Harper - 'The Harpie'. She talks well, debates better and has made a few of the cabinet look like dummies, which indeed some of them may be. Keep going with your other lines of enquiry of course. We are not taking sides but have a rifle through the Harpie's past as you do so. If anything detrimental crops up, so be it. If not, no harm done. Any other members of the shadow cabinet you happen to cast a forensic eye over might prove fruitful too. Our patron would appreciate this little favour. Obviously this conversation never really took place."

"I'll see what I can do," promised Bert, fairly sure he wouldn't do anything much different from his current plans. He had dismissed Harper from his list of possible targets a long time ago. She had grown up in care and survived both physical and sexual abuse as a child to excel at school. Beating the trend again, she won a scholarship to Cambridge and gained a first in Politics, Philosophy and Economics. She turned down a job offer from a leading merchant bank, which she obtained just to prove that she could, and worked for a homeless charity while canvassing for her local Labour candidate in her spare time.

Thereafter she gained the chance to stand in a no-hope constituency for Labour and won it, to the surprise of everyone but herself. She was popular with everyone but the government and had never been involved in any unsavoury dealings that he could uncover. He had no intention of wasting any more time looking for dirt that he was sure wasn't there. Stories of her being abused had surfaced first in her own autobiography and improved her popularity with her supporters no end. It also meant that trying to score cheap points against her became a losing game for her opponents. Bert had no intention of making the same mistake.

Chapter 29 – Mac and John the Beast on Duty

As the days dragged on, the strange household settled into a routine of sorts. Since the arrival of the gym equipment, the men spent a lot of time using it, both to stay fit and to relieve the boredom. Two of them were always on duty at the radios and printers: Sue assumed that each one would make sure the other stayed awake as there was very little in the way of radio traffic. The packaged composite or 'Compo' rations were replenished weekly by the anonymous looking transit van, but the group had also started to enjoy fresh food too as a result of Sue and Sandy's regular trips to the local convenience store. The fresh air seemed to suit the twins who slept better, to everyone's relief.

The manager of the local store now welcomed them whenever they entered his shop, assuming them to be a nice new couple, recently moved to the neighbourhood with their twin sons. This natural error suited all concerned, although Sandy started to amuse himself by invented a whole history for himself and Sue. She found herself slowly but surely becoming a fascinatingly exotic creature, having been born in Japan, lived in the USA, where the twins were conceived before they had been born on a steamer between Australia and New Zealand. The owner of the shop listened to the snippets of stories each time as Sandy let his imagination run wild. On a visit during the second week of their stay Sandy went too far and when he started telling the owner about meeting Sue in a brothel in Singapore she kicked him hard on the shins. After he squealed in pain she said quite gently, "Stop your teasing, honey. You know that isn't true."

Back at the flat when Sandy complained publically about the bruise on his leg, Old Bob took him aside and told him to wind his neck in or he'd get more than a kick on the shin.

The addition of fresh fruit and vegetables along with milk, decent coffee and chocolate bars cheered everyone up, even if the pressure on the two toilets in the property didn't let up much. Like some legendary Blackpool boarding house it was decreed that the men could pee in either toilet but for Sue's benefit they would only use the downstairs one for anything more solid, to keep the smells at bay.

One night, Mac and John had stagged on at the radios which, as usual were almost entirely silent. John had a book as was his habit but Mac was bored and wanted to talk to help pass the time. Only Mac would have been reckless enough to keep interrupting John's concentration while reading after it had been made perfectly clear that was what he wanted to do.

“What are you reading?” asked Mac in an attempt to start a conversation.

“Fuck off,” said John, knowing Mac didn’t care.

“Do you think we’ll be here for the rest of our lives or will something happen sometime soon?” asked Mac trying a different tack.

“Fuck off, I’m reading,” said John in a more menacing tone.

“So why did you do selection?” asked Mac, seemingly encouraged by the responses so far.

“To see the world. Now fuck off, I’m reading.”

Mac was encouraged that John was now starting to answer his questions, after a fashion. He bent down and read the cover of the book.

“Crime and Punishment. So, is that a detective story?” he asked.

John looked up and stared at him in a way that would have made anyone else leave him alone. It had worked for years in pubs, airports and restaurants. Mac, however, was both fearless and relentless.

“The last book I read was a western.”

John ignored him.

“Want to know what it was about?”

“No,” said John.

“It was about a gunfighter,” said Mac.

There was no reaction.

“It was called…”

John still tried to ignore him but his concentration had been ruined.

“The Grapes of Wrath,” said Mac.

“That’s not a western. It’s one of Steinbeck’s greatest works.”

“There’s a gunfighter in it though.”

“No there fucking isn’t,” said John who put down his book, signalling to Mac that he had won.

“Is it the one with the elephant?”

“Fuck off and leave me alone,” said John who had lost any chance of concentrating on his book.

“Now you’ve put that book down tell me; why did you join The Regiment?”

“Same reason as you probably,” said John.

“Nobody liked you in your own regiment.”

“Okay, so it wasn’t the same reason as you. But now that you have ruined my evening I’ll tell you, if you promise that if I do you will shut the fuck up and let me read till the end of this stag.”

“Sure, sure,” said Mac unconvincingly.

“I wanted to help people and keep them safe, know what I mean?”

Mac nodded, just pleased that he now had someone to talk to. The topic was irrelevant to him.

“Have you ever read ‘Catcher in the Rye’?" asked John.

“Yes,” lied Mac.

“Well that’s me. Keeping people safe from falling over the cliff; watching from the edge of the field of rye.”

Mac hadn’t a clue what John was talking about, but he seemed intrigued by John’s genuine concern for humanity. Up and till then he had assumed that he was in it for the excitement, travel and the chance to kill people with government approval.

“So you really joined to help keep people safe?”

"Yes. When I left school my only success had been stopping the bullies from picking on other kids. After I'd beaten them up a bit and told them to behave, they all did. It was my personal anti-bullying policy. I never got into school work at the time so career options were limited. I joined my local regiment to serve in Northern Ireland and after two tours getting abused by both sides, did selection to keep the whole country safe."

"You're kidding me?"

"You asked so I told you. We are in this unit to protect the public; with our lives if necessary. It's just anti-bullying on a bigger scale."

"But how do you know if we are actually doing that or just being used as window dressing for some ponce of a politician?"

"Every day that there is no terrorist attack is a success against the bullies. After the Iranian Embassy siege nobody fucked with Thatcher's Britain for ages because they knew they would get a doing. We are the playground monitors at the moment and if anyone starts anything we'll finish it. We are keeping all the civvies safe. All the men, women and children going about their daily lives. Your wife and kids; Sue and the twins."

"But you'll never know if we actually are. The only way we would know for certain is if some bastard showed up and threatened them in front of us, which is not about to happen. If they did I'm with you sorting them out, no hesitation, but otherwise we have to believe what the lying thieving politicians tell us."

"You'll know if you're doing the right thing, trust me," said John picking up his book again, indicating that the conversation was over as far as he was concerned.

Mac seemed deep in thought by his standards.

"I just joined to pull birds," he said, almost to himself. "Still, I'm glad we had this conversation."

"Fuck off, I'm reading," came the reply.

Chapter 30 – The Whip's Hand

Sir Geoffrey was in his own office one day catching up on constituency mail when the phone rang. It was Sir Crispin Jessop.

"I wondered if we could meet up and look at the awkward squad before tonight's vote on benefit reform. Are you free?"

Sir Geoffrey had been putting off the routine correspondence for weeks now but jumped at the chance to avoid it further.

"I could pop up now if you like. How many are we looking at?" asked Sir Geoffrey.

"No more than a dozen by the look of it, but with the majority as slim as it is we need to lean on a few today to make sure we win the vote tonight. The opposition have approached a few of the rebels and smell blood."

"We can't have that. I'll come up and you can tell me if the PM needs to phone anyone personally."

With that, Sir Geoffrey closed down his desk-top computer, put on his jacket and headed for the Chief Whip's office. When he arrived he found Sir Crispin pouring over a spreadsheet like a general considering the map of a battlefield.

"There are fifteen actually who have said they will vote against the second reading tonight. A number which means we will lose. I think the PM might be able to persuade three of them who feel they still have a chance of advancement in the future."

Before Sir Crispin could say anything else, his mobile rang and his eyes lit up.

"Really? Good, don't let them leave even if you have to break their legs." He finished the call and looked round at Sir Geoffrey. "Four of the bastards are having lunch together in Portcullis House and I have enough dirt on each of them to stop them in their tracks. Would you mind waiting here till I sort them out? This four plus the PM's three should be just enough."

Sir Geoffrey nodded his agreement to wait and took a seat while Sir Crispin beetled off to help stem the rebellion. While he waited, the PPS looked round Sir Crispin's office, largely out of boredom. He had been there so often he never gave the décor or layout any thought. He found the dark arts of the whip's office distasteful and tried not to get drawn into the detail of their work whilst in their lair. He stood up and walked over to the window and watched the water of the Thames flow past, with boats flowing with it or making slower headway against the current. A metaphor popped into his head which he mentally noted for his memoirs and then he turned away from the view toward the desk and Sir Crispin's spreadsheet.

It was an A3 sheet with every politician in the parliamentary party, minus the cabinet, who were assumed to be loyal in any three line whip. If not, then the task of bringing cabinet members to heel fell to Sir Geoffrey or the PM. This was a very rare requirement, due to the inherent ambition of most ministers. The spreadsheet was headed with the details of the bill and against each name was a tick or, in fifteen cases a cross, written in pencil. Sir Geoffrey recognised the names. Three were regular trouble makers with no ministerial ambition, while the rest were in marginal seats who feared for their jobs at the next election if they supported this particular bill.

Sir Geoffrey's gaze fell on the briefcase beside the desk. He recognised it as the battered old case Sir Crispin kept close to him at all times, even in Dudley's. Rumour had it that it contained, amongst other things, a notebook detailing any indiscretions by MPs in the party which could be used to influence their voting intentions. The word blackmail was never used to describe this process but blackmail it was, pure and simple.

He was not, by nature, nosey or a gossip, but he found the temptation to have a look inside the case irresistible. It might be the only time in history that Sir Crispin had ever left the case unguarded and thus the contents of his notebook available for inspection. It had only happened due to a combination of his eagerness to collar the four rebels having lunch nearby and his trust of Sir Geoffrey.

Sir Geoffrey looked at the clock. Only fifteen minutes had elapsed since The Chief Whip had left; perhaps sufficient time to have reached Portcullis House but nowhere near enough time to lean on the traitors and return, even with Sir Crispin's legendary abilities. Sir Geoffrey decided that if anyone should know the contents of The Chief Whip's case and notebook it should be the PM's Parliamentary Private Secretary.

He made sure the office door was fully shut and returned to the desk where he opened the briefcase. Inside was a surprisingly neat array of paperwork, mainly in manila files, a tablet and beside those items, in a separate section an aging address book.

Sir Geoffrey removed it carefully and unfastened the elastic band which kept the yellowing pages firmly shut.

After guiltily looking over at the door he opened it at A. The first page was headed with Benjamin Alcot, a backbencher from the South West, elected for the first time at the most recent General Election. Underneath it were the words ‘drink’ and ‘women’ followed by ‘no details’. That was hardly earth shattering news he thought. Benji Alcot had been caught out often enough and was rarely completely sober, even at the start of each day's business, assuming he showed up at all.

He opened the book at random and found an entry under Edward Jones which read; ‘young boys, file B1257’.

"I wonder where that file is," he wondered to himself. There had been rumours about Jones but nothing in the press. The entry suggested that a detailed file existed somewhere which contained details of indiscretions which could be used to bring Jones into line if he ever waivered.

A sudden thought struck Sir Geoffrey and he opened the book at S, where he found on the fourth page, an entry under his own name. It read ‘affair and child, HP resolved at time.’

Sir Geoffrey closed the book in shock. What the hell did that mean? Nothing had been done by anyone other than Nicola who withdrew from politics and quietly had the child with her parents' support. Nobody had had to do anything, and who the hell was HP?

It didn't take long for the penny to drop. HP. Sir Henry Pearson, the Prime Minister's father, had been Chief Whip at the time Geoffrey was first elected. What had he done? How had he resolved things? Things had resolved themselves when Nicola had been killed by the driver, no doubt drunk, in that hit and run.

Geoffrey sank into Sir Crispin's chair. "Good Lord," he thought to himself. What if it hadn't been an accident after all? The powers that be at the time had seen a danger to their sparkling new government and had brutally removed it. The more he thought about it the more he became sure of what had happened. The child had miraculously survived the impact, cocooned in its pram. Presumably with Nicola dead they had decided the child was insufficiently dangerous to risk a second 'accident' and had left it to grow up in peace.

"What a fool," he told himself. He knew Sir Crispin was an absolute bastard but it was a shock to find that the PM's father, Henry Pearson, had been an absolute bastard from the same mould, or was at least prepared to go along with something like this. The PM's father was dead and had been for eight years, his funeral conducted with the pomp and circumstance befitting a career politician who had fathered a political dynasty before retiring to private life without a blemish against his character. Tributes had been paid by politicians past and present extolling the virtues of a fine man and a wonderful father. Geoffrey suddenly wondered how many had been thinking all the time about the notes in a similar notebook held by Sir Henry.

Sir Crispin had taken over as Chief Whip some years after Sir Henry, in a natural succession largely unreported at the time during a cabinet re-shuffle.

Chapter 31 - Domestic Bliss

Sue was struggling to open a jar of baby food when one of the guys walked through the kitchen behind her. Frustrated at the tight lid she held it above her shoulder and shouted, "Help!"

A hand took the jar from her and handed it straight back, loosened.

“Thank you,” she shouted and looked round to see John the Beast walk through the other door.

"Why can’t every woman have half a dozen strong men about the house to open jars and fix things for them?" she thought to herself. That wasn’t even taking into consideration the sexual possibilities which had to be better than Brian’s recent efforts. An even more appealing prospect if Jason ever took an interest in her.

Later that day Sue had been aware that the twins had been crying again but was also aware that she was ‘Stood Down’ and that somebody else was scheduled to deal with them. Despite her growing confidence in the men’s abilities she was still as concerned as any mother would be if strangers were looking after her children. As a result she couldn't help peeking through the gap in the bathroom door to watch. When she did she saw Mac standing with the twins on the change table in front of him. On the other side of the table the three younger men were watching him attentively. Sandy even had a notebook in his hand.

"Most of the time the baby functions quietly enough but will cry when either hungry or the nappy is full," said Mac. "Immediate action drill is therefore to check the nappy. If it is clean, evidenced by a lack of smell, the baby is hungry and should be fed. I will cover that in the next lesson."

Sue watched in awe as Mac covered all the essentials of changing a baby's nappy as if he were instructing the soldiers on one of the weapons they had to use and maintain. Mac saw her watching but continued as if she wasn't there.

"The first stage is to remove and dispose of the contaminated material. Watch closely how I deal with the first one as I will get one of you to deal with the second."

Sue felt a pang of concern as she realised that Mac was talking about her children but from the grip he had on Ben it was clear he was in no immediate danger. Mac continued the lesson by removing the nappy and placing it in a nappy sack with surprising dexterity, suggesting this was something he had done many times. All the while he described in soldier-proof language what he was doing and the dangers of getting it wrong, something he referred to as chemical contamination. He continued by cleaning Ben thoroughly, though gently enough, and finally fitting a clean disposable nappy.

"Any questions?" he asked when he had finished. Debbie and Ray shook their heads, indicating they had understood what was required. Sandy checked his notes before asking; "What if you're in the field and you don't have all the kit you need?"

"Then you improvise. Any clean cloth will do and any clean bag you can seal will do for disposal. Never leave base without enough nappies though. S.O.P.s."

Sue recognised the oft used abbreviation for Standard Operating Procedure having heard it a hundred times already. She always translated it now as "do what we always do". She watched, fascinated as Mac ordered Sandy to change Joe's nappy. She half expected Mac to use a stop-watch to time him but he didn't. He watched carefully and only commented when Sandy got poo on his hands trying to put the old nappy in its sack while simultaneously holding a wriggling Joe on the table. She hoped that Joe's first words would not be any of the ones Sandy used at that point. After ten minutes or so, both babies were returned to their cots, clean, happy and smelling human again.

“Job done, lesson learned,” said Mac as the men headed back to their previous tasks.

"Maybe she had misjudged Mac after all," thought Sue, although she still wouldn’t like to get into an argument with him.

Chapter 32 - The Jessops on the Rise

At a quiet table in Dudley's, Sir Crispin Jessop and his nephew James were enjoying a relaxed lunch together. It was a Saturday and the club was fairly empty at lunchtime compared to its usual bustle during the week. Both had ordered the steamed fish and both were regretting it but their meeting had nothing to do with the abilities of the weekend chef.

"I keep hoping Old Sore Throat will land a decisive blow on Pearson at PMQs but he seems supremely able to snatch defeat from the jaws of victory each time," said James.

"I am afraid I have to agree. Even Brian Smithe could have been more effective recently and that is saying something," replied his uncle, abandoning his assault on the fish in favour of the remaining vegetables.

"I would get rid of Smithe in a shot, given half a chance" said James changing the focus slightly. "His family never spelt their name with an e you know. They probably couldn't afford the extra letter. He added it when he stood for parliament thinking it added some kind of weight to his name. Nothing spells trade quite like the name Smith, wouldn't you say?"

"No doubt," replied Sir Crispin. "However, you shouldn't get rid of such a useful punch bag until it's absolutely necessary. The press love ripping into him because it is so easy and this takes their focus away from more important members of government. He is very useful chaff in that respect. Anyway, I didn't invite you here for lunch to talk about Brian Smithe, with or without an 'e'."

"Nor for the delights of the steamed turbot, I assume."

"Certainly not," said Sir Crispin pushing his plate forward in a sign of defeat to the waiter. "I invited you here as I feel the time is fast approaching when young Pearson will need to be replaced. The figures don't look very favourable as far as a second term are concerned and he won't be allowed to continue if he loses to Eddie Benton."

"We have to find a way of making Benton unpopular with the electorate and we need to do it soon. It doesn't seem to matter what he does or says; his supporters love him."

"My dear boy, you can be so naive at times. Yes, we need to find a way of removing Eddie Benton; that much I agree, although I don't think he will last much longer as party leader, even if only through extreme old age. But the last thing we want to do is do it soon. It would rather suit our purposes, (and by 'our' I don't mean the party's purposes), if young Pearson ploughed it at this election and had to be replaced by a younger and more able minister such as yourself shortly thereafter. Benton won't make it to the following election, especially if it is the full five years later and the younger replacements all look like 'Blair light'. Admittedly The Harpie is more able but she is too volatile to lead the party effectively."

"You really are a devious bastard, Uncle," said James with obvious admiration in his voice. "So we let Charles lose to Benton and then I step in to his shoes in time to beat Eddie's replacement after he chokes on a Wurther's Original."

"Something along those lines, but I have an insurance policy in hand to end young Pearson's political career even if he manages to win, which is not beyond the bounds of possibility, given Benton's faltering performances of late. I suspect he is more likely to choke on a soother than a Wurther's Original. He should certainly give them a try for that bloody cough."

"So we let things take their course, and either Charles flounders at the General Election and needs to be replaced or he wins, and then some political disaster befalls him and he has to be replaced anyway. You must be pretty sure of what you have about him?"

"Oh, don't worry on that score. I have been saving something rather juicy about the Pearsons for ages. It will make smoking pot and the pig's head look like a pimple on an elephant. I can't go into detail, but suffice to say that their tax affairs over the years would make very interesting reading. Add to that a rather peculiar hobby of our PM in his early days as an MP and he would be off like a shot the minute it became public. Either way it is important that we are seen to be entirely loyal and supportive of our boss in the run up to the election and we ensure that nothing appears out of the woodwork which could be blamed on us in any way. We need our actions to appear consistent and give you the springboard to surviving young Pearson's demise before reluctantly taking over his job. Coffee? I don't think I'm brave enough to face this chef's take on Eton Mess."

Chapter 33 – Brian Receives an Ultimatum

Brian Smithe had not been looking forward to the phone call to Sue. He had tried to convince himself that she would agree that it was best all round to call it a day and for her to accept a settlement which would allow her to raise the twins without any financial problems. That wouldn't stretch to private schooling or anything like that. It was a struggle enough to afford it for his existing children. If she knew she had a house to live in and a generous payment each month he felt she might accept an amicable split.

He was surprised to find that her mobile was unavailable when he tried to contact her. This annoyed him considerably, as he had to leave a message each time rather than deal with the problem with his courage built up. After leaving five messages over a period of three days he was caught off guard when Sue finally returned his call, as he had feared, at a highly unsuitable moment. Brian and his own wife had just met the chairman of his local party committee and his wife for a tour of The Palace of Westminster before lunch on the banks of the Thames when Sue called.

Brian’s face fell and he mumbled an excuse for calling back later that day but Sue was having none of it.

“I assume from your stammering you’re with your wife or somebody more important than me, but listen, and listen carefully. If I don’t hear an announcement in the press that you are leaving your wife for me and the twins by the end of the week, I am going to the press myself. I gather some of the Red-tops will pay handsomely for an exclusive low-down on a story like this. The twins will be provided for one way or another; either you do the decent thing or I’ll do the dirty on you.”

With that Sue ended the call.

Brian forced a smile on to his face and pretended to finish the call at his end.

“I have to go now, Sir Geoffrey, but leave that to me,” he said to the inert mobile in his hand.

As he put it back in his pocket and recovered his composure he joked, “I’m afraid The Chief Whip takes priority over even you, my dear, when one is a minister.”

The local party chairman and his wife laughed politely, proud that their man was indeed a cabinet minister.

Brian’s wife, though, didn’t laugh. "The caller certainly seemed to have you worried," she thought to herself having noticed the call end earlier than her husband had indicated. "Maybe the rumours are true then."

The rest of the day was purgatory for Brian as he simultaneously tried to charm his guests, ignore his wife's enquiring glances while also trying to think through how to deal with Sue's ultimatum. The afternoon seemed to last forever but eventually it was time for his wife and their guests to head off to take in a West End show while he returned to work.

As soon as he got to his office he tried to phone Sue but was frustrated to find that there was again no reply. He was frantic with fear. He knew from her tone that Sue had been serious about what she had said. It was unlikely that she would even listen to an offer of financial assistance in her current mood. He was also now sure that his wife suspected something was going on and he would be forced to face an inquisition when he got home, even if he managed to delay that till the early hours. He could fend off one but not the other, and he briefly wondered if it wouldn't be easier if he just set up home with Sue and damn the consequences. Even as he thought through that option he remembered he would then have to deal with both Sir Crispin Jessop and Sir Geoffrey Stanning. He immediately dismissed that option and poured himself a large scotch.

After a moment or two's consideration he decided that if The Party wanted his support in all things he needed its support in return. He slowly and reluctantly picked up his desk phone and asked for the Chief Whip's office.

Chapter 34 – Cobra 2

As the various professionals arrived for the next COBRa meeting they were, without exception, badly pissed off. They had attended one meeting where a real and present threat was outlined by the security services and had gone back to their respective offices to ensure that London's emergency services were at peak readiness to deal with anything and, hopefully, from a police perspective, actively working to prevent a spectacular attack from happening in the first place. Their work had been hampered throughout by political interference which included unattributable press briefings confirming that at least one highly trained SAS unit was deployed in the capital ready to kill any terrorists at a moment's notice.

When the Met Commissioner had gone on record not only saying that he didn't think the SAS presence was necessary considering the training of his armed officers but also hinting that it was a political stunt to gain public support, the unattributable briefings switched to the question of his age, imminent retirement and competence.

The press had dutifully covered all this with relish, but some had focused more effort on tracking down pictures of 'Our brave lads from the SAS' ready to risk their lives to defend London's citizens. The hundreds of policemen prepared to do exactly the same thing went largely unreported.

As a result of all this the meeting began in an atmosphere of tension. The heads of the emergency services had been in daily contact and had their staffs at a high state of alert, but were all aware they couldn't continue this indefinitely. The head of the Army had been kept in the loop but only just; Police primacy was something very dear to the heart of the Commissioner. The Commanding Officer of the SAS had remained in London for weeks now but had had to stop the free movement of his team leader between briefings and the safe house due to the investigative activities of the press. All these people had believed the attack would have happened by now or have been stopped by the actions of one or more agency. Instead the PM's focus was almost entirely on how to deal with the public's disappointment at the lack of action to date.

He began by thanking all the heads of the organisations present for their hard work to date and almost apologising that there had, as yet, been no test of their preparations. He asked for a brief update from each as to their state of readiness and any information which they could share with the assembled group.

Only the head of MI5 was able to add a vague update, informing everyone that his sources suggested that the terrorists appeared to have delayed their activities and that he believed the specialist timing devices were still a long way from London, although he could not provide any further information on the whereabouts of the main cell members.

The meeting descended then into what the Commissioner hated most: a largely political discussion about how to take the credit or pass the blame should anything occur, good or bad. At one point even he was shocked at how crass the conversation between the political members at the table became.

The PM's press secretary seemed worried that the public might approach the General Election thinking there was no real danger from terrorists and questioning the recent interruptions to their lives.

"If we don't have terrorists for the SAS to kill there must be somebody else?" he asked in mock seriousness.

"The Speaker?" suggested The Home Secretary in jest.

"At least that would enjoy cross-party support," said the PM before realising the humour was not impressing the heads of the emergency services. “Let’s not take this matter lightly, gentlemen. These are the facts: we know there is a terrorist cell in or near London with explosives they are prepared to use against innocent members of the public. We know that the final member of the cell is in Scotland with the necessary timing devices to put the plan into operation. Despite exhaustive efforts on all our parts, we have not yet located the main group and are now wholly reliant on keeping tracks on the final group member to track them down. We have The Metropolitan Police at High Alert and a specialist team from the SAS on standby. There is also an election in two months’ time. Have I missed anything out?”

The Commissioner was about to add that the government were also five percentage points behind the opposition in the opinion polls but thought better of it. With nobody adding anything else the PM called the meeting to a close after asking that everyone redouble their efforts in tracking down the cell and thus safeguarding both the population and the present government.

Chapter 35 - Bert Butterfield - Closer

Despite a natural reluctance to be steered in any particular political direction, Bert Butterfield felt a hint of duty, if not to the owner of the paper, at least to his editor who signed off his, often very large, expenses claims. As a result he went home from their meeting and started to Google 'Dawn Harper' for a while as he drank a mug of dangerously strong coffee. His enquiries confirmed what he already knew about her early history and indeed her meteoric rise within the shadow cabinet. Any digging regarding her political career confirmed just one thing: she had got to where she was based on merit alone. She was brighter than her peers, more committed and more genuine than anyone else in parliament. Nothing of any use to a tabloid journalist then.

He had read her autobiography and it modestly backed up his estimate of her abilities and character. She had been abandoned as a baby and then adopted by a couple who were then deemed unsuitable by her local authority when she was three years old. Thereafter she grew up in a succession of care homes, some of which were later revealed to be worse than any choice of family settings.

She had suffered both physical and on one occasion sexual abuse and was open about it to reassure others in the same position. Despite this she excelled academically and had made it, to date, to the level of shadow Minister for Families.

Bert was about to give up and start surfing porn when he caught sight of an article in the local paper from Dawn Harper's home town which included an interview with a former school teacher. He had to read it several times before he realised what had seemed out of place. The teacher, who may have been privy to reports which she should have kept confidential, had complimented her prodigy on overcoming the loss of her mother as a child to achieve so much. That was not quite the story in Dawn's autobiography, where she said she had been abandoned. It was a slight difference on the face of it but if the teacher was correct then it was the only occasion he could find where 'The Harpie' had not reported the exact facts. It may be nothing, he acknowledged, but if she had blurred the truth about not knowing her mother then perhaps there was a reason. It wasn't much, but he decided to check it out anyway.

The article in the local paper was ten years old and the teacher had been retired at that time. After a bit of leg work he found that she was still alive and was living by the seaside in Margate. His professional curiosity aroused, he took a trip to the seaside and tracked down the former teacher in a small cottage close to the sea-front. He arrived late morning and found that there was nobody at home. As it was raining, he waited in his car until a tiny woman returned to the house, carrying a gym bag with a badminton racquet sticking out of it and walking at a pace which completely belied her seventy years. He gave her a few minutes to settle into the house than walked over and rang the doorbell. The door was opened cautiously with a chain securing it from forced entry.

"Yes?" she said suspiciously when she saw Bert.

"Hello, Mrs Miller?" Bert asked.

"Miss Miller," she corrected with the effortless habit of a lifetime.

"I'm Bert Butterfield. I'm a political... writer and I am writing a book on women in politics. I wondered if you could spare a moment or two to chat about Dawn Harper in her younger days. I believe you once taught her."

Miss Miller eyed him up and down, suggesting he was not the first journalist she had met wanting to know about her most famous ex-pupil.

"I have given all the interviews I intend to give about Dawn. You can Google all the previous ones and get what you want, I am sure," snapped Miss Miller.

"I understand," said Bert smiling and turning on his charm. "It must be getting annoying to be pestered all the time, having produced such a successful politician. As a woman it must be great to see her providing such a positive role model for other girls to emulate."

Miss Miller stared at him looking for a hint of flannel or sarcasm but could detect none. She had rather liked the suggestion that she had been a major influence on Dawn.

"I'm not sure I can be credited with any of her subsequent success, Mr...?"

"Bronson," lied Bert effortlessly, using the first name to come to mind. "I am sure all teachers think that way, but I remember the ones who influenced me while I was at school and often wish I could meet them again and thank them."

Miss Miller was starting to relax a little so Bert pressed on.

"The book I am writing is about influential contemporary women who could help girls who are perhaps unimpressed by the heroines provided by popular culture. The book is being funded by a successful woman herself.

It is not designed to make money. I am not at liberty to say who exactly but suffice to say she has encouraged more children to read books than any other person I can think of. I believe she is something of a hero in the eyes of many teachers. I can't promise a mention in the credits as it is under her control, but she does have a soft spot for teachers, especially female teachers who have influenced others in a positive way."

At some point while Bert was saying the above, Miss Miller seemed to change her mind about giving an interview and let him in. He accepted the invite immediately before she could change her mind. Inside he found himself in the neatest and cleanest house he had ever seen. Even the furniture seemed to be set out in straight lines.

Bert accepted the offer of a cup of tea and found it served in a proper teacup and saucer, something he hadn't experienced for years. The whole visit was like taking a step back in time.

"Do you keep in touch with any of your former pupils? Dawn or any of the others?" asked Bert in an attempt to loosen Miss Miller up.

"A few by email and facebook. Dawn always sends a Christmas card but recently it is printed rather than signed personally. I don't mind really though; it's so nice to be remembered at all after all these years."

Bert smiled his warmest smile.

"Was she your star pupil, then?"

"She has done well so far, especially considering the difficult start she had in her life, but I taught a few others who have turned out well too. There were some doctors, a few nurses, a magistrate and a lawyer or two. I taught at least four who became teachers. They tend to keep in touch although the job has changed considerably by the sound of it. I'm glad to be out of it really."

"I've read all I could find about Dawn, and impressive reading it makes too. I wondered if she showed early signs of the greatness to come?"

Miss Miller eyed Bert carefully and seemed to decide, for whatever reason that she could trust him.

"She was always very focused on her school work, that's true, but she cared about lots of other things too. I gave her detention once for refusing to remove a CND badge from her blazer. The school's rules stated no badges but she was adamant on her principles and wouldn't budge. In my early years of teaching she would have been caned but that would have done no good either. In the end we agreed she could pin it to her school bag. If I hadn't compromised I'm sure now she would have spent every day in detention rather than stop displaying her beliefs. She also cared about others. It was never just show. She would go out of her way to welcome any new pupils even if they were awkward or unpopular - in fact especially if they were outsiders. It was very noticeable. I admired her although her stubbornness knew no bounds. I'm sure you've heard these things before. Much of it comes through in her autobiography and in other accounts of her early life."

"Yes indeed, but it is refreshing to hear it first hand from someone who has known her for so long."

Miss Miller seemed to be warming to her subject but Bert was keen to bring her back to the matter of Dawn's mother.

"I have read both that she was abandoned at birth and that her mother died when she was very young. Dawn wrote that she was abandoned, so I guess that's what happened."

Again Miss Miller paused and sized up her visitor. The sense of caution had returned but he managed to dispel it again with a well practiced smile.

"She always regarded herself as having been abandoned, and may even have started to believe it. She always felt abandoned anyway, but her mother didn't abandon her. The report I read from social services made that clear.

Her mother had been killed in a car crash, I think. No, it was a hit and run, now I think about it. Dawn could only have been months old at the time and never knew her father."

"So she never met any of her family at all?"

"Not as far as I knew," said Miss Miller. "Actually that is not strictly true. There was a cousin of her mother's who happened to work in social services who followed her progress. It was very much against the rules as the initial adoption was meant to be secret, but she came along to a number of school concerts that Dawn was in. I always thought it nice that a relative was there on such occasions. Dawn met her briefly after one of the shows but never knew who she was."

"That was nice," said Bert. "You don't remember the cousin's name do you?"

Miss Miller started dredging through her remarkable memory.

"Miss Joyce. Thelma Joyce. Her father was the brother of Dawn's mother's father, if that makes sense, so they were quite close relatives in a way."

"Bingo," thought Bert. So Dawn Harper was born Joyce. Possibly Dawn Joyce but Joyce for definite. Now to track down the family.

"Do you know if the cousin ever got in touch?" asked Bert.

"Not that I was aware of. She was very strict about the rules and was worried that even I knew she came along to the school. It was our little secret. More tea, Mr... ?"

Bert had completely forgotten what surname he had used and after a moment of panic replied, "Yes please, and it's Bert. Please call me Bert. Don't worry Miss Miller, I won't give away the secret. Unattributable source and all that. I am pleased that one member of her family had seen her success though."

Miss Miller smiled and poured him another cup of tea.

"Thelma came to the school a few times on a professional basis involving other problem children on the Social Work register. Not that Dawn was a problem child really. She'll be retired too, I think, now. Last I heard she still lived in what is now Dawn's constituency."

Bert had been taking notes and underlined the sentence "Thelma Joyce, Social Worker, second cousin". He also ringed the name Joyce.

After a few more general questions which confirmed to him that Miss Miller had no more information of use to him he politely made his excuses and left the retired teacher's house.

Back in the car he reviewed what he had discovered. The Harpie had not been abandoned, at least not by her mother, but had been orphaned by a tragic hit and run. It wasn't scandal, he had to admit, but there was a whole new story here if he could track down some real family members. If he could also track down the driver of the hit and run that was a headline. He had to admit that was too much of a long shot, but you never knew in this business.

Chapter 36 – Jack Hunter's Farewell

Over the years Jack Hunter had been asked to do many things. Often it was simply warning journalists or whistle-blowers that they had to keep their mouths shut or they would face prosecution under the Official Secrets Act. Whatever they were about to expose was a matter of national security and any publicity would be bad publicity. He noticed a pattern with the secrets he was tasked with, ensuring they remained secrets. They were nearly always indiscretions by public figures: MPs, Cabinet Ministers, judges or senior policemen. Most involved sexual activity with minors. At first he was uncomfortable with the nature of the work but slowly and surely he stopped caring. Twice he was ordered to accompany Smith and another man while they visited a police station and impounded files, again on the pretext of protecting National Security.

He had also been ordered to stand guard outside a flat while Smith and the other man, introduced only as Brown, paid a visit to a person of interest. It wasn't until two months later that Jack noticed in the local press that the person of interest had died on the evening of the visit, and although the coroner had recorded a verdict of natural causes on the death certificate, the man's family were convinced of foul play. So was Jack, but as an accomplice, he wasn't going to raise his suspicions with anybody.

He found that his already heavy drinking had increased to the level where any married person, or someone with concerned friends, would have been advised to seek help. Jack fell into neither category and continued with excessive consumption of whisky on a daily basis. As a result he occasionally found himself receiving instructions from Smith whilst very drunk. It had led to one instance of him receiving a chase-up call when he had failed to carry out the task, so he had schooled himself to write everything down, no matter how illegible it was the following day when he awoke.

It was one such note which reminded him of a call the previous evening when Smith had called in a state of unusual panic. The task had been a quantum leap beyond anything Jack had been asked to do before, but apparently there was nobody else available and Smith needed him to act swiftly first thing the following morning. The scribbled note contained an address in Cricklewood and the description of a woman who lived there with her twin babies.

Jack read the next part again: "Kill all three and dispose of their bodies in deep woods somewhere. No fuck-ups."

As he re-read the note he sobered up far quicker than usual. It was one thing to be an accessory to a possible murder which was being covered up by the full weight of key members of the London establishment: it was quite another to be asked to kill a woman and her children in cold blood, alone, and then dispose of the bodies. Jack was not at all happy with this request. On the rare occasions previously where things had got heavy, he had had the safety of knowing that both Smith and Brown were with him and taking the lead. He had a plausible defence in claiming to be an undercover member of Special Branch who was acting under orders, unaware of the full actions of his superior. This task was a different matter entirely. He would be acting alone, killing three people using a gun which he knew had no serial number, on the telephone instructions of someone he already suspected was a hit man of one sort or another. If anything went wrong he could be left carrying the can with no real means of identifying or implicating Smith or Brown, whatever their real names happened to be. More likely still was the possibility that he would come to a sticky end whilst in custody, long before he had a chance to spill any beans in public. He wasn't sure what to do and would have dearly loved to pour himself a large whisky and hope the whole situation disappeared in a drunken haze.

He had been ordered to carry out the killings by midday at the latest, and it was already nine o'clock. He showered quickly and dressed in an anonymous suit and tie before pocketing his warrant card and gun and heading for his car. He kept it in a lock-up nearby along with various tools he thought he might find useful in his current line of work. In the lock-up was a large roll of polythene which he had found in a skip one day and shoved in his boot with no real expectation of it being used. It now seemed to be a requirement for this task if he went through with it as ordered. He put it into his boot along with a large joiner's saw and a smaller hacksaw. He shivered a bit as he did so but for now it was good to keep busy. He had convinced himself that he would make a final decision during the journey to the house as to whether or not he would actually kill the family group. He could still pull out of it and make a run for it; London held nothing of value for him anyway. He had money in his suit and money hidden in a bank account, with an alias he was sure would stay secret even to Smith. He could survive on that for a long time till things died down and he could start afresh.

There was the nagging thought in his head that if this hit was so important and if he didn't carry it out then somebody else would, sooner or later. After that he would be the next on the list as a liability to all concerned. By this reasoning it might be better to buy himself some time by alerting the woman to the danger and taking her and her children as far from London as possible. He could then report the job done to Smith whilst making more detailed plans for disappearing for good. On balance this last option began to sound like his best course of action. He resolved to do just that. Break into the flat and sneak the targets out disguised as corpses, having warned the woman that it was her only option. If anyone was watching he would make sure he lost them on his way towards the New Forest. Then he would head north to a large city and drop her off with a wad of cash and a warning to stay out of sight as long as possible.

By the time the money ran out he would be in Europe with a new identity and would take his chances thereafter. Whatever happened to the target and her kids after that would be her problem and not the result of direct action on his part.

As he headed off towards the address in Cricklewood he was really no further forward as to what he would do when he got there. He normally drove with the radio on but switched it off straight away for this trip. He needed to think, and inane chatter and bland pop music wouldn't help.

When he reached the address he had been given he passed the mews property and went once round the surrounding area to make sure there were no police or public around who could interrupt his activities or his get-away.

After parking his car nearby, he took the roll of polythene from the boot and walked the short distance to the house. Placing the polythene down, out of sight of the door, he took his gun from his pocket and rang the doorbell.

....

....

Inside the house Sue and the men from Jason's team were going about their routine, bored but keeping as busy as possible to pass the time. Just Steve was on duty with the twins; Debbie was on radio watch and the others were busying themselves with the gym equipment or cleaning dishes and weapons.

When the doorbell rang it took everyone by surprise. The soldiers certainly weren't expecting any visitors and neither was Sue. She was sitting on the sofa with Steve watching the BBC children's channel CBeebies, while they each rocked one of the twins in baby bouncers using their feet. Disco Bob sat beside them cleaning a shotgun and checking cartridges, each of which appeared to have one large ball-bearing ready to shoot out the end. He was trying not to make it too obvious that he was also trying to follow the programme on the television.

The sound of the doorbell made everyone sit up and reach for a weapon, with the exception of Sue, who reached forward and pulled the twins closer to her. Mac was nearest the front door and signalled for everyone to be quiet by placing a finger over his lips. Sandy came through from the kitchen and asked what was happening. Mac ran a finger along his throat which Sue guessed either meant Sandy had to shut up or that Mac was going to cut his throat later for making a sound. She decided either was possible.

John moved to join Mac near the door while Disco Bob and Sandy moved quietly to cover the back door. Everyone waited for the bell to ring again expecting whoever it was, parcel delivery at the wrong address or Jehovah's Witnesses targeting the least receptive house in the neighbourhood, again. However, the bell made no further sound. Instead those nearest the door could hear the sound of somebody placing a key or pick into the lock.

Mac and John exchanged looks which suggested they both found that a little unusual, and they moved to take up positions either side of the front door in order to deal with whoever appeared, while closing over the door to the lounge. Eventually the lock gave way and the door opened slowly. A hand moved inside the door with Jack Hunter following on behind. As he entered the front hallway he felt a gun press against his neck as a large figure whispered in his ear. "Give me the gun."

Jack slowly turned round with the gun hanging limply underneath his hand. As he did so he caught sight of John the Beast.

"Shit," he thought to himself. "That's not Sue White."

Mac appeared from his other side and Jack realised he was caught between two ruthless killers. Then he believed the penny dropped. His bosses had been worried he might chicken out and had tasked these two to carry out the killings. Either that, or they were playing it safe with belt and braces, tasking both him and these two thugs to kill Sue and the twins, knowing one would succeed.

He should have kept that thought to himself and let his captors speak first but he was so overcome with relief that he had been handed a way out of his dilemma that he tried being a bit too helpful.

“Look, if you’re here to kill the woman and her twins too, that’s fine by me. You take the money and I’ll just head off home. In fact if you need it…”

Without thinking he leaned outside the door and grabbed the roll of polythene, completely ignoring the gun a rather confused John was pointing at him.

“…you can use this to get rid of the evidence, as it were. I won’t need it now.”

“That could be really useful,” said Mac with a smile. “So you were sent to kill Sue and the kids too, were you?”

“Yes,” said Jack, by now euphoric as the relief cursed through him.

"All professionals together," he thought, "working for the same team."

He’d be home and starting to get drunk an hour from now without having to hurt anyone.

With John still covering Jack from the right hand side of the door, Mac stepped over to the living room door and closed it fully.

“Give us a hand opening up some of this stuff, mate. Best if nobody through there watches it getting prepared. Know what I mean?” said Mac with a wink.

“Sure,” said Jack. I give them a quick hand with this then off home and leave them to it.

He turned to look at the huge figure of John the Beast behind him who was fixing a silencer to his pistol. John winked a conspiratorial wink which reassured Jack enough to let him concentrate on helping Mac unroll a length of polythene.

“Three sections or just one big piece?” he asked Mac.

“Just one big piece should do it,” replied Mac as John pulled the trigger behind Jack’s head.

Chapter 37 – A Trip To The Woods

Inside the living room, everyone waited with bated breath. They could hear voices in the hallway but couldn't make out the details. After a few minutes there was a soft plopping sound which the soldiers recognised as a shot from a silenced gun, followed immediately by Mac sticking his head through the door and telling them to relax but stay put. Used to doing what they were told in strange and dangerous circumstances, they stayed put but stayed tense with their weapons to hand.

Out in the hall Mac and John looked at each other. There was no panic in the glances they exchanged, just a momentary questioning of each other as to what the next step should be.

Mac broke the silence first as he started searching through Jack's pockets, looking for his car keys.

"I'll find his car, you wrap up the body."

John obviously decided this was the best course of action and quickly gathered up the plastic sheeting where Jack and his spilled blood had landed. Mac found the car keys and disappeared outside, returning after five minutes or so.

"His car's outside, it was parked close by," said Mac, as he and John quickly lifted the large package and carried it to the open boot of Jack's car.

"Tell the guys I'm stir crazy and gone for a drink," said Mac. "I'll be as quick as I can."

John had placed a folding spade from somebody's rucksack on top of the body in a moment of inspiration and Mac indicated he had noticed it.

"Sure," John agreed quite casually.

Mac jumped into the car and drove off.

Without looking around to see if anyone was paying attention to what had happened, John quickly joined the others in the lounge.

"Everything okay?" asked Steve in a worried tone.

"Sure," replied John calmly. "Mac's gone for a drink. The boredom's getting to him. He'll be back in an hour or two I guess."

The others looked concerned, especially Steve, but they were more concerned at Mac going off the deep end, and those who had worked with him before knew that a few beers would relax him without any effect on his abilities.

"He shouldn't have gone. Anyway, I thought I heard a silenced shot," said Steve.

John looked at him for a few seconds before saying, "He was most insistent when I tried to talk him out of it."

There was a pause while everyone including Steve weighed up the situation.

"Fair do's, but Old Bob will shoot HIM if he isn't back when we need him."

Everyone slowly returned to what they had been doing before. John breathed a sigh of relief and hoped Mac would remember to smell of drink when he returned from disposing of the body and the killer's car. On that score, he needn't have worried.

Mac headed north out of London as quickly as the traffic allowed. He wished he had been heading out of Glasgow into the surrounding countryside which he knew well. This was all Englandshire as far as he was concerned and might as well have been Basra for all he knew about the green spaces he was heading for, but at least heading north cheered him up. There was, however, one exception to that: he and two of the guys had spent a mind-numbingly dull month covertly spying on a suspected terrorist arms dealer in woodlands in Cambridgeshire. Nothing came of it apart from a stinking cold but he remembered the area and the routes in and out of the OP. He headed for that as the only bit of the English landscape he knew well enough to use to hide a body.

After a frustrating journey swearing at every car in front of him, he arrived and was relieved to find the area near the large mansion was as quiet as he remembered it. He parked off the road and managed to drag the body out of the boot and into the wood. An hour of digging produced a fairly deep hole for the body and he tipped the bag in, before filling it in again. As an infantry soldier he had always hated filling in trenches and this was no different. He worked as fast as he could and then covered up the area with branches as best he could. He then disguised the large marks from dragging the heavy body and sped off in the car.

The return journey seemed quicker and he reached an area of wasteland he had spotted on the way out of town after a total of four hours, forty five minutes away from the house. The team were on six hours' notice to move, meaning if the shit had hit the fan the moment he had left, he had just over an hour to torch the car and get back to the safe-house. He looked round and confirmed nobody was around. He had been relieved to find the car was petrol engined and he quickly rigged a fuse into the fuel tank and lit it, running for the nearest corner as he did so.

There was a whoosh behind him as the car went up in flames but he didn't look round to admire his handiwork. He half walked-half ran the journey back, depending on whether there were people about or not, constantly checking his watch as he did. The last part of the route he did walking casually, drinking a can of super lager he had bought in an off sales. It had been a risk, he knew, but how suspicious would anyone be about a sweating jock buying a single can of super lager 400 miles from home? Not very, he decided.

He let himself in through the back door prepared for a scene of chaos in the house and a severe bollocking from Jason or Old Bob. Instead he found Debbie making a couple of mugs of coffee in the kitchen and John, Sue and Steve watching the news on TV.

As he walked into the front room, he finished the can of lager.

Steve looked up and asked, "Feel better?"

"Much," said Mac.

"Whatever happened tonight better not happen again. Understand?" said Steve.

"Don't worry, it was a one off."

Chapter 38 - A Bit of a Cough

Eddie Benton reached the Houses of Parliament on his bike and got off. He was surprised at how out of breath he had become and found himself wheezing a little bit as he bent down to take off his bicycle clips. This had happened a few times recently and it had concerned him more than a little. He accepted the fact that he wasn't getting any younger but this had been a fairly rapid decline in his breathing beyond simply the aging process. He had also been suffering from a niggling cough which refused to go away. It wouldn't have bothered him as much if it hadn't become a feature at the end of speaking. Almost like a form of punctuation. This had been seized upon by the awkward squad in parliament on the government benches who had even started parodying him and mimicking his cough when heckling him. Some journalists had picked up on it too, suggesting it was perhaps a sign of nerves. Eddie knew it wasn't, but it didn't help his party's standing, coming on top of what was seen by many as some lacklustre recent performances against the former captain of Eton's debating team, the Prime Minister.

He made his way to his parliamentary office and went through the mail and the plans for the day including his questions for that day's Prime Minister's Question Time. Throughout the meetings and conversations of the morning he was very conscious of the cough interrupting and punctuating his sentences. His staff and colleagues were also aware of it, to the point that his closest friend and shadow foreign secretary took him aside at one point and suggested he stood in for Eddie.

Eddie smiled and reassured him all would be fine. But it wasn't. PMQs offered the opposition the chance to attack weaknesses within the government over both benefits and Europe and he had a raft of difficult questions lined up. It should have been a good day for the leader of the opposition but he found himself coughing at just the wrong times and came across as hesitant and nervous when he knew he needed to be seen as anything but. The backbenchers opposite him started their childish coughing routine and for the first time it rattled him. He was trying to follow up a question on European security when he even had to stop and cough mid-sentence. As a precaution he pulled out a rather grubby looking handkerchief, eliciting loud laughter from the back benches. Things got worse though. As he coughed into it he was shocked to notice blood amongst the mucus and completely lost the thread of his question. He stumbled to a vague question which the jeers from the government seats suggested had left the PM untouched.

For his part the Prime Minister was relieved not only to be getting an easy ride regarding difficult issues but also to find his usually well versed opponent having a complete off day. As Eddie mumbled to a conclusion the Prime Minister rose to his feet, sensing blood.

Chapter 39 – Breaking up the Happy Home

Sue woke with a start to find John the Beast's face close to her own, aware that she had been tapped very gently on the shoulder. He placed a mug of tea beside her on the bedside table along with two digestive biscuits. His actions were gentle and calm, clearly designed not to disturb the sleeping twins, and completely belied his size and power. After her initial shock she stared at him with a questioning look.

"We're off," was all he said.

"Off?" asked Sue, trying to wake quicker than usual . "Off where?"

"The job's on, so we have to go."

"Who has? What, all of you?"

"Yes. All of us."

"When will you get back?" asked Sue, as if they were all off to the office for a standard eight hour day.

“We won’t,” said John before putting a hand on her shoulder. “We had a whip-round to help with the twins. It’s not much but hopefully it will make things a bit easier once we’ve gone.”

He handed over a bundle of notes that looked as if everyone had handed in all the money they had in their pockets. She guessed there was a couple of hundred pounds in the roll.

“Thanks,” she said struggling to take in the finality of the words.

As he rose from the side of the bed John turned round and handed her a small slip of paper.

“That’s my mobile number if you have any more trouble or anyone threatens the twins. Okay?”

Sue nodded and smiled. He still looked terrifying but she was cheered up by the offer and very glad he was on her side. With that he was gone.

Sue finished the tea and pulled on her dressing gown. The twins were still sound asleep and she saw from her mobile phone, which had mysteriously returned, that it was five o’clock in the morning. Suddenly she wanted to thank all of the soldiers for their kindness, and she rushed downstairs. The lounge was empty of people and kit. The radios were gone, along with the kit bags and any trace that the house had been occupied by seven other souls for most of the last five weeks. As she went through to the kitchen she saw that all the dishes were cleaned and had been put away. She just caught the garage door being locked and the sound of a transit van pulling away before realising that she was indeed alone again with Ben and Joe.

Chapter 40 – Job Done !

As soon as Jihadi Jock left Glasgow the 'Alert' state went through the roof within every agency involved in providing security for London. Jason was briefed and told to get his team ready to move, and if necessary go into action from a standing start. He had already reduced their notice to move from six hours to one and knew they would be good to go. There was a strong likelihood that they would have to take out the entire terrorist cell with little or no time to plan an assault on any safe house being used. He and old Bob returned to their own safe house and quickly briefed the troops on what they knew, which now included photos of the entire cell.

Existing half sections made last minute preparations and checks, together with confirmation of roles which had been tried and tested to the maximum in preparation for just such a requirement. All equipment was loaded into the two vehicles; the Range Rover would lead with Old Bob, John the Beast, Mac and 'Just' Steve ready to pursue and if necessary stop any vehicle. Jason and the rest of the team were in the transit van which could inconspicuously approach any target or property and if necessary drive them to a rendezvous with the police at an incident without raising suspicions.

When everyone was ready and the vehicles prepared and double checked, Jason put the two kettles on so everyone could have a brew while they waited. Each with a mug of tea or coffee in their hand, they sat in the lounge, dressed in black flame resistant suits, with balaclava masks rolled up above their faces chatting as if about to watch football down the pub, but with their guns beside them or on their knees.

They all knew it could be a long wait even at this heightened state of alert, or it could be a false alarm. It could even all happen without them. Either way there was nothing to do now but wait.

After two hours or so Jason's mobile rang. He wrote an address on a page of his notebook twice and tore the page in half as he listened to the rest of the orders from his CO. When the call was over he turned to the rest of his team.

"We're on. Jock's arrived in London and has taken a cab from Victoria to a greasy spoon where he is currently eating a very non-halal breakfast. We're going to this police station where we come under the control of the Silver Commander there."

He handed the two slips of paper to the drivers and turned to John the Beast.

“You have ten seconds to tell Sue we’re off.”

John quickly picked up one of three freshly made mugs of tea along with a couple of biscuits while the others checked they had all their kit and made for the vehicles.

Once there the drivers keyed the address of the police station into the Sat-Navs. Debbie opened the garage doors as quietly as he could and as soon as John returned and climbed into the Range Rover the vehicles drove out. Debbie closed and locked the garage again and they were off.

They sped through London quickly and arrived at the Police Station fifteen minutes later. A uniformed Police Officer was standing at the entrance to the car park, clearly expecting them. He indicated that the vehicles should head for the rear of the car park, where another officer removed cones from two large spaces which the drivers were able to reverse into.

Jason and Bob jumped out and the rest waited in the vehicles. Mac rolled up a jumper and, using it as a pillow, got comfortable and tried to sleep. There was a bit of chat in each vehicle but not much. Mostly the men were alone with their thoughts. All keen to get stuck in, shoot some bad guys and live to tell the tale, no doubt over and over again.

Jason and Bob headed for the back door of the station where a uniformed sergeant met them and said simply, "This way."

They followed him through the corridors of the police station and up a flight of stairs till they arrived at a control room. There a female chief superintendent introduced herself as the Silver Commander for the incident.

"Welcome on board," she said without any emotion. "What do you know so far?"

Jason quickly covered his briefing to date and that he was now under police command should they need him and his team.

"We have every firearms officer in London on duty now and armed response teams throughout the capital. Intelligence have said they reckon the cell is somewhere in my patch, and apart from yourselves I have three hundred armed officers at my disposal. With a bit of luck you can have a cuppa or two and head home. Jock is still finishing his second full English. Looks like he is making sure he wasn't followed. If it were up to me I would have lifted him by now and made sure he doesn't get the timers to the rest of the group. If they are in this area we have enough police around to see them make a runner. Anyway, it isn't up to me. From what I can make out there is a lot of political involvement here, so God only knows what will happen. It's Jane, by the way."

"Jason, and this is Bob," replied Jason as they all shook hands. "We'll both stay here for now. The lads are ready outside."

"Sergeant Wilcox here is your liaison for admin. If you need anything while you're here: brews, food or the loos, just ask him."

"Cheers," said Bob who headed over to get to know their brand-new friend.

Chapter 41 – Soft Cell

Ahmed Khan couldn't quite finish his second cooked breakfast. That final sausage and some beans had defeated him. He sipped at his third cup of tea and looked out of the window of the café/diner. There was nothing untoward outside as far he could see. A few people passed either on their way to or from work but it was still early. Inside a few tables had customers sitting having a bite to eat, including a table with three cab drivers chatting loudly about last night's football and this morning's customers so far. He had plenty of time yet. All he had to do was get to the address where the rest of the cell were waiting, hand over the timers and get back to Glasgow. Whatever happened thereafter was somebody else's problem, or at least that was what his handlers had led him to believe.

When he finally finished his tea he picked up his ruck-sack and used the toilet. It was filthy and smelled of at least one cab driver's early morning bowel movements. It was all he could do stop throwing up while he emptied his bladder. After washing his hands and deciding the towel would negate the effect of the soap and water he left the toilet and headed to the cabbie's table.

"I need a cab. Any chance?"

One of the drivers agreed and asked for the address. He nodded to confirm he knew where it was. It was a relatively long trip and would be a good fare to add to the night's business before finishing. He finished the conversation he had been having with a final insult about West Ham, and headed out to his cab with Khan in tow.

The cabbie started a conversation with a few questions about football, and was pleased to find his fare happy to chat and to join in with some banter on the merits of football north and south of the border. As they sparred with each other both failed to notice the second black cab which had followed them as they left the diner. Missing that, they had no hint of the three police armed-response vans following the cabs, out of sight but aware of their every move.

Back at Silver Command, Jason and Jane watched the progress of the convoy on the large screen in front of them. As the vehicles moved, others were moved strategically around in their wake and those watching speculated about the final destination. Jason couldn't help but notice that the route was bringing them closer to the station where they were standing. Not quite being handed the terrorists on a plate perhaps, but with a bit of luck bringing them conveniently close.

When the cab was only a quarter mile or so from the police station, the vehiclefollowing reported it had abruptly slowed and pulled into the side at a bus stop. After a pause, another report confirmed that Khan was out of the cab, had paid the fare and appeared to be standing waiting for a bus.

“Is there any chance he has explosives as well as the timers and is carrying a bomb already?” asked Jason.

“My understanding is ‘no’, but I’ll ask for confirmation and permission to pick him up now.”

A quick message to Gold Command received a swift response that he did not have explosives and had to be left to join the other members of his cell, even if he got onto a bus, crowded or otherwise.

Jane shrugged and Jason shrugged back.

Khan let three buses pass him without making any sign of planning to get on. One of the officers at the control centre confirmed that the three buses covered all the routes from that stop. He wasn’t waiting for another route. A report came in that Khan had started walking northwards away from the bus stop. After ten seconds another message informed those watching that he had suddenly turned round and started walking the other way. After a further pause a breathless voice managed to report that Khan had turned down an alleyway and was running when the follower got sight of him again. Jason heard street names mentioned and instructions shouted to the following vehicles before the breathless voice came on again.

"Shit, he's gone into 47 Thackeray Avenue. Semi detached, two floors. Curtains are drawn on all windows."

The map over on a screen to the right of the main incident monitor homed in on Thackeray Avenue and surrounding area. Jason looked at its location, noting that it was a short road with junctions at both ends giving a total of five other connecting roads. Two of them were cul-de-sacs, the others gave way to further routes away from the area. He turned to see Jane bringing armed units in from all directions and quickly sealing off the property. The units also sealed off the roads which the garden of number 47 backed onto. A cordon of four properties either side and across the road was marked on the board with units readied to remove all possible civilians from the properties swiftly on Jane's command. While this was happening she was briefing her Gold Command on the state of play and asking for authority to raid the premises. Jason was impressed. He had trained and trained with some of the Met's specialist officers and knew they were more than capable of kicking the door down and taking care of half a dozen terrorists, armed or otherwise; looked like he and his team could soon go home. He knew the guys would be disappointed, but they would also all be alive.

After a pause authority was denied and Jane was told to put Jason on the secure phone.

Jason heard his boss's voice at the other end of the line.

"The powers that be want you to go in and deal with whoever you find inside, and they don't want anyone making it to court afterwards. Understood?"

"Yes, Sir," replied Jason as his adrenaline level rocketed.

As he finished the call Jane nodded to confirm that she had had similar orders from her chain of command although hers had not contained the 'no prisoners' aspect.

"I've been told that because of the chance of the bombs now being complete you are to go in rather than us. The PM doesn't want dead coppers on his watch but you are expendable."

"I suppose we are," said Jason calmly.

"There are two cars outside which will escort you there. We will start evacuating the residents from the furthest away houses the second you are on the ground. I don't want a blood bath outside number 47. What you do inside is your business."

As Jason nodded and headed off with Bob she added, “Good luck!”

At the vehicles the guys were all wide awake, having been brought up to speed by Bob on their own radio net throughout the unfolding situation. All the vehicle radios had been switched to the police frequency for the incident. Jason gathered the men together around the transit van and briefed them quickly on the tasking. There was no time for a detailed recce and planning. This would have to be a quick assault based on standard operating procedures. In other words, Old Bob and Debbie would fire stun grenades into upper windows at the front and rear respectively as a distraction. Then John and Mac would kick down the front door and go in firing while Disco Bob and Just Steve would do the same at the back. Once the front door was clear Ray and Debbie would take the stairs with Jason covering them. Outside Sandy Shaw would cover anyone leaving the building without permission at the front, with Old Bob doing the same at the rear.

“Questions?” asked Jason.

“No, Boss,” came the reply from the other members of the team.

"All being well, we'll be back in Hereford for Tea and Medals by dinner time," said Jason and they all climbed into the vehicles.

The driver in the leading escort vehicle had obviously grown up watching The Sweeney and tore through the streets of London. The Range Rover could keep up on the straight, although it struggled to corner at those speeds, but the transit van had no chance. Eventually Jason had to get a message through to him to slow down a bit. The car did so and as they reached Thackeray Avenue it pulled over to one side, letting the following vehicles pull in beside the mobile command unit parked in a driveway slightly out of sight of number 47.

Jason and Old Bob climbed into the back of the unit and found a uniformed Chief Inspector who was the Bronze Commander waiting for them. He confirmed the evacuation of neighbouring houses had started and that he had snipers now covering any possible exit from number 47 or its garden.

"I've been told they may have assembled the bombs already," he said to Jason.

"So have I," came the reply. "We'll move along to the garden of number 45 now. Once we're there I want no police in 47 till I say so. If I can't then Bob here will be in charge. And make sure your guys know anyone wearing a black suit like this and a respirator is a good guy."

"Will do," said the Chief Inspector before adding, "Good luck."

As Jason left the vehicle, the Chief Inspector's mobile rang and he was surprised to find himself speaking to the Commissioner of the Metropolitan Police. Iron Mike was calm but measured in every word he said.

"I want you to be quite clear on this one John. I don't care how disappointed the armed response guys are, they leave this one to the army. There is a strong chance of fatalities on both sides and I want every one of my coppers to go home alive today. Got it?"

Bronze Command said he had.

"If the army don't sort it themselves we will do this by the book as a hostage situation or whatever it becomes, but none of my bobbies get hurt."

As soon as he had acknowledged the order the chief inspector's phone went dead.

Chapter 42 - Eddie Gets Some Bad News

Edward Benton had lived a healthy life. He was a vegetarian who only occasionally weakened and ate some chicken or fish. He had never smoked; well, never tobacco anyway, and was such a rare drinker that there were press pictures of almost every pint he had consumed over the last twenty years with constituents. He cycled everywhere he could and had often gone on cycling holidays with his wife and children. These days he had extended this to his grandchildren. If his lifestyle was ever documented in a medical journal it would have had a tick in every box for ensuring the maximum chance of a long and happy life. He was unlikely to contract any of the main killers of adult males in the United Kingdom, going by all the statistics. If sixty percent of cancers were caused by lifestyle choices he was living a life which should have avoided most of them. Unfortunately, Eddie fell into the forty percent group who were just unlucky.

The niggling cough had got progressively worse and he knew it was affecting his performance as party leader, especially in parliament. His wife had grown concerned too and had eventually insisted he saw a doctor. She had noticed that Eddie had lost weight recently and as there was little spare flesh to start with she didn't want to lose any more of him.

After a delay to ensure he fully met his political duties, including his weekly local surgery, he managed to fit in an appointment with his GP. The doctor checked him over thoroughly and confirmed that he was in good nick for a man of his age or even one ten years younger. There were a number of explanations for the cough he had been experiencing, most of which were minor ailments and would either go away of their own accord or could be treated with a course of drugs. The appearance of blood when he coughed was of more concern though. There were a few other possibilities which were highly unlikely but to rule them out, as much as anything, Eddie's GP advised a series of tests be carried out and suggested he went private to speed things up and make it easier for Eddie to keep the process out of the press. Eddie insisted that he received no special treatment and seemed unconcerned if the press found out about a series of routine tests. His press officer would have had quite different views, already at full stretch to reassure the voters that his aging boss would make it through a full term as Prime Minister if elected.

The GP submitted the necessary request for tests and both waited for a suitable appointment to be arranged.

Almost two months later Eddie headed for his local hospital with his wife and went through a full CAT scan as well as taking along samples of most of his body's finest products. He managed to ask the staff a range of questions about themselves and their work, confirming his fears about the state of the NHS and the morale of those working within it. By the end of the visit he had largely forgotten about the real reason for being there.

He returned to work the following day and carried on as usual, fairly certain that the tests would come back confirming one of the minor problems outlined by his GP as being the cause of his recent health concerns.

He was surprised to have a call from his GP put through to his office the following day during a meeting with a female shadow cabinet colleague, despite leaving instructions not to be interrupted. The doctor had a tone in his voice which immediately alerted Eddie to a serious reason for the personal call. The doctor was nervous and Eddie wanted to put him at ease.

"Just give me the details, please; I would prefer to hear whatever you have to say by phone now."

The doctor cleared his throat and told Eddie that he had lung cancer, that it was quite advanced and inoperable. After a prompt from his patient he added that he needed to undergo chemo-therapy and take a complete break from work. Even if he did there was no guarantee of success. In short, he should prepare himself for having only six to twelve months to live. They made an appointment to meet the following day before Eddie rearranged it so as not to miss Prime Minister's questions and then he hung up.

His colleague looked at him with genuine concern.

"Nothing to worry about," said Eddie. "Men's problems."

The two finished their meeting and Eddie phoned his wife when he was alone. She took the news quite badly and he promised to get home early that evening if possible so that they could discuss it together. When he had finished that call, Eddie turned his chair so that he could look out of the window. Unusually, he took in none of the view.

There was an element of inner rage at the nature of his illness. He had never smoked and had kept himself fit as few his age had managed. The doctor had explained that although lung cancer affected smokers most often, it was not uncommon for non-smokers to contract that form of cancer too especially if they had spent time in smoky atmospheres. He thought back to his years in the smoke-filled rooms of his constituency, talking to the local party stalwarts who shared his political passions if not his views on a healthy lifestyle. He remembered many of the people who had helped him in his early years, most of whom were now dead. He could smell the rotten smell of cigarette smoke in his clothes and hair after meetings or evenings listening to people in the pubs and clubs of his constituency. For a brief moment he hated them all for what they had done to him. But it was a brief moment of self indulgence and he dismissed it from his mind, feeling annoyed more with himself for such a moment of weakness.

"So this is it," he thought to himself. All the effort to help people over the years and the improbable chance of the top job snatched away at the last minute like a cruel joke. Had it all been worth it? How would people remember him? The best Prime Minister they never had, or a joke in his own right? Having had the unexpected chance to steer the direction of his party towards everything he had always believed in would it now be lost?

As ever, the speculation gave way to a reasoned process. How could he ensure that redirection became a lasting one for the party? He went through in his mind the manifesto for the next General Election and wondered if he could write a forward so stirring to the party faithful that it would change their thinking for generations to come. On balance he thought that beyond his abilities. He thought of his unfinished autobiography, with its deliberate honesty, and immediately worried about the spin doctors in the government pouring over it after his death to discredit everything he had managed to achieve, little as that was to date. The more he considered the problem, however, the more it all boiled down to one thing. Who would replace him as party leader?

At home that evening, after he had calmed his wife and reassured her that he was strong enough to face it, they spoke for some time about what they should do with whatever time he had left. There were family details to sort out, including when to tell their two children and at what point to tell their grandchildren. They decided to leave the informing of grandchildren to their own children to decide. Other financial matters were discussed and decided before they focused on the implications for Eddie's political life. The couple had always worked as a team since they met at university and this was a time to continue that approach if ever there was one.

In essence they agreed that he would continue as if all was well for a month or so while looking very closely at his shadow cabinet colleagues to see who would be most likely to continue his work. Once that had been decided he would take a few colleagues into his confidence and prepare the chosen successor as best he could for a further two months or so. When he felt they had the best chance possible he would go public with his health problems and resign from the leadership to allow the election of his successor. From that point onwards he would spend what time he had left with his wife and family, making himself available to the party if they wished to consult him. He refused to consider any form of treatment until that work was done and after an hour of trying to change his mind on this matter, his wife gave up, recognising in her husband the determination he had in some things which not even her influence could change. Once all these decisions had been made he and his wife went to bed with two mugs of cocoa as usual and each read a few pages of their books till sleep appeared inevitable and they both switched off their separate reading lights.

The following day Eddie went into his office and got on with business as usual. He was not on the best of form at Prime Minister's questions but that was hardly out of the norm and he chaired a rather mundane meeting of his shadow cabinet where he deliberately left most of the talking to the other members in order to start to gauge their abilities as leaders.

His closest friends in the shadow cabinet tended to be of a similar age, and while able in many ways, they were likely to succumb to a similar fate to him sooner than the party could withstand. Of the middle ranking members with some experience behind them, he found many enjoyed the trappings of power too much to be trusted with the direction of policy after he had gone. There were a few younger ones there but they were a bit raw and would have been chewed up and spat out by the Prime Minister in any head to head across the despatch box. The exception to all of this was Dawn Harper.

She was young and relatively new to politics but she had shown character from the day of her maiden speech. She cared nothing for the trappings of power, only for what the wielding of that power could achieve for the people she represented. She was a passionate and very able debater who had put even the PM on the back foot on more than one occasion. In every respect but age she was the natural candidate.

Eddie made a point of having more private meetings with his shadow cabinet colleagues than usual over the next few weeks. During these he listened to their views and assessed them from the perspective of a potential party leader. Few measured up to the standard which he believed was necessary and there were indications from some of the more ambitious ones that they might change back to a more centrist route for the party if given half a chance.

Dawn remained an exception to all these fears. He found that they were very much on the same wavelength on all the main issues with a common approach on how to get there. The main difference he perceived was her energy levels and ruthless impatience to achieve results. This he saw as a danger to her success in the role of party leader. She was as likely to advise civil disobedience in the face of government legislation as to advocate measured argument in parliament against it. While he admired it and remembered the three times he had been arrested during anti-apartheid and CND protests he knew it would finish her chances of leadership at an early date; and it would have to be an early date if she was to replace him.

Dawn was slightly suspicious of Eddie's attention when she found herself in his office alone for the third time in the space of ten days. As an attractive young woman in what was still essentially a man's world, she had been subjected to unwelcome male attention all too often. While most occupations would have sweeping redress for some of the sexist comments and behaviour she had been subjected to, politics seemed to be exempt from these norms. The awkward squad from the government had called her things and suggested things which would have resulted in an easy victory at an employment tribunal in any other circumstances. Instead they were cheered on by their leadership, if not live on television, at least behind the scenes. Nor was the problem limited to any one party. She was completely teetotal but found herself regularly trying to lobby colleagues in the evenings on important matters when they were half cut. On several of these occasions she had been propositioned by married men in the division lobbies or in the bars of parliament. It had happened often during her brief council career and she could handle it easily enough, but she was disappointed to experience it again here. When she confided in a more experienced female MP from her party she was met with a shrug of the shoulders and a 'boys will be boys' reply.

Eddie had never before engaged in any such behaviour and she didn't really expect it now, but he was taking an unnaturally close interest in her these days. She entered his office warily now but found nothing to raise her suspicions further. On the contrary he always seemed to be obsessed with policy and strategy, seeking her opinions in a way which few others did. She would relax to a large extent and tell him how she felt the party should be proceeding and give her honest opinions about friend and foe alike. Eddie would listen carefully and probe further or urge caution where he saw her entering dangerous ground.

All fear regarding his intentions was dispelled however, when he asked her out of the blue to have Sunday lunch with him and his wife the following weekend if she had nothing else arranged. Having something else by way of a private life was a joke she didn't share with him on that occasion. She lived for politics and spent all her time away from parliament in her constituency, working or reading. She had no private life to speak of and Sundays were often spent impatiently waiting for the working week to begin.

She accepted the invitation gratefully and looked forward to meeting the very private and reputedly quite shy Mrs Benton.

When Sunday arrived Dawn took a taxi to Eddie's house in Notting Hill. He had lived there since getting married and had seen the area change out of all recognition during the forty years he had lived there. As a result he now lived amongst affluent Tory voters in a house worth a small fortune, simply because he had bought a modest house in the area where he had grown up and felt at home. She doubted if he felt as at home now.

Mrs Benton, Rose, welcomed her at the door and apologised for her husband not being there to meet her as he was on the phone to the BBC answering a question relating to the PMs' appearance on that morning's Andrew Marr Show.

She accepted Rose's offer of tea and they chatted for half an hour before Eddie appeared. During the time they chatted, Dawn was surprised to see how informed and passionate Rose was about her husband's work. They were obviously a team and while Eddie was the public figure, his wife was as much a part of a joint effort to pursue their common goals.

When Eddie arrived he apologised unnecessarily and joined the conversation. Dawn was relieved that there was no patronising comment about women's talk or such like. Instead Rose quickly briefed him on where the conversation had got to and he joined in. If the press officers and advisors could have briefed as economically as Rose did then, Dawn thought, she could save an hour a day easily.

Lunch was a pleasant, modest nut roast in keeping with the vegetarian nature of the household and Dawn was again relieved to find it was home-made and rather tasty. The conversation ranged over family issues, world events and the government with a relaxed ease and Dawn found herself in the unusual position of feeling quite at home. She offered to help wash up and when the offer was readily accepted, she found herself drying dishes while the leader of Her Majesty's Opposition, in an old apron, washed them. The conversation continued as they worked and she felt quite guilty about ever suspecting Eddie of having any ulterior motive for inviting her to his office so often. He was obviously that rare beast: a genuinely happily married man, and this gave him the stability to endure anything that his opponents in parliament or the press could throw at him.

After several coffees Dawn reluctantly said she had to leave and prepare for the week ahead. She thanked Eddie and Rose, giving Rose an instinctive hug as she left and almost doing the same to Eddie. In the taxi on the way back to her flat she felt better than she had for some time. It had been a very pleasant afternoon and if it became a regular feature in the years ahead she decided she would like that very much.

Once Dawn had left, Eddie and Rose sat down each with a herbal tea and shared their feelings. Both had been impressed by Dawn's commitment, knowledge and passion. She was reminiscent of them both in their younger days but with the killer edge which they had lacked. That was probably why she was already in the shadow cabinet and being reported in the press on a regular basis. The key question they each had was whether that edge would be to her advantage or not if the leadership was thrust upon her at such an early age. On balance they decided it would. Dawn was as staunch a believer in the cause of socialism as they had ever encountered, and it was clear she would never be tempted to the dark side by the wealth and trappings available to her if she compromised her principles. No they agreed, there wasn't a drop of Tory blood in Dawn Harper.

Chapter 43 – Tea and Medals

Once Jason and his team were in position things moved quickly to a conclusion, as far as those watching outside could tell. They heard two bangs, one from the front and another from the back of the house, quickly followed by the sound of smashing glass and the sight of smoke puffing out of the upper floor. Almost simultaneously the locks of both the front and back doors were hit by solid rounds from shotguns before the doors were kicked aside and figures clad in black suits and gas-masks rushed in. More noise followed as stun grenades went off, followed by a barrage of shots from small arms; then three quick shots in a row. There was a short pause before a further round of gun-fire. After that everything went quiet for a few seconds; then two shots were heard. Thereafter silence returned. The police marksmen watching outside breathed a sigh of relief. No bombs had gone off and as far as they could tell, no innocent civilians had been hurt. True, they had not been able to fire shots themselves, but they had been ready to and would go home with stories to tell.

Inside the house things were very much more animated. Once the stun grenades had gone off and the door-locks shot away the entry teams rushed in ready to shoot any figure they found. Although they were prepared for the fact that the bombs could have been assembled and detonated as the assault began, instead they found a scene of relative domestic calm. Jason's team soon put a stop to that. John and Mac found the hallway empty and stormed into the lounge covering each other as they went. There they found three figures who had been watching Predator on the television until the stun grenades broke their concentration. Two were holding cans of super lager while one had a bottle of cider sitting on the table beside him. All three were shot twice before they could move, two by John the Beast as he barrelled through the door and one by Mac as he joined him in the lounge. They checked the room and satisfied themselves that they had got everyone in that room. Mac moved back to the door and gave the next group a thumbs-up. Ray and Debbie raced up the stairs while Jason had a quick look at the three figures slumped in the chairs, looking as if Predator had either put them all to sleep or scared them to death.

"Make sure they don't move," said Jason and headed after Debbie and Ray to cover the assault on the upper floor.

As he left the lounge Mac shot each of the figures in the head, picked up a can of super lager, removed his mask and took a long drink.

"That wasn't really what I meant," thought Jason, realising what had happened behind him.

At the top of the stairs, Ray had kicked in the door of the first bedroom and gone in shooting, Debbie was covering his back while also watching the doors of the other two bedrooms and the bathroom door, which was closed.

Ray shouted, "Room clear," and reappeared at the doorway. As he did Debbie started towards the next bedroom but the door opened before he reached it and a female figure came out holding a gun in front of her. Debbie shot her before she could level it at him and he rushed past the falling body into the room.

"Room clear," he shouted to Ray and Jason.

The door of the bathroom suddenly opened and Jason fired three shots as a figure emerged desperately trying to do up his belt and zip. The unarmed man slumped backwards dead, with the words 'What the…" strangled before he could finish them.

Ray kicked in the door of the third bedroom and fired shots at the bed and the bigger cupboards before returning to the doorway and confirming the room was clear.

While the lounge and upper floor were being cleared, Disco Bob and Just Steve charged through the back door and straight into the kitchen. There they found Ahmed Khan and another figure waiting for the kettle to boil. The look of surprise on their faces didn't last long as Bob shot them both twice in the chest. As Jihadi Jock's colleague fell to the floor a pistol fell from his belt, making a loud clatter on the tiled floor. Bob kicked it towards the back door and moved to the door which connected the kitchen to the lounge. He heard Mac and John the Beast deal with the occupants of that room and shouted through that the kitchen was cleared. Mac acknowledged and confirmed the same for the lounge. After a minute Bob heard a further three shots from the lounge. He popped his head round the corner, his pistol ready in his hand. Instead of resistance from the terrorists he found Mac sitting on an armchair with his mask off and a can of beer in his left hand, his pistol still smoking slightly in his right.

"Everything okay?" asked Bob.

"Yep," Mac replied. "Beer?"

"Maybe later."

Shots rang out upstairs and Bob and Steve headed for the hallway to join Ray at the bottom of the stairs. Ray signalled for them to wait with him as shots rang out in short bursts with pauses in between. After each burst, the three heard the words "room clear" with nothing to indicate casualties amongst their colleagues upstairs. The shooting stopped after a few minutes and Jason came to the top of the stairs.

“Three dead here and the rooms clear. Loft’s empty too. Ray, give them a hand upstairs checking for explosives and booby traps but it looks like we caught them with their pants down; one literally.”

Jason, Disco Bob and Steve returned to the lounge to find John poking at Khan’s rucksack and Mac finishing a can of lager with his gun pointing needlessly at the three corpses in front of him.

“Can I leave these three now and help with the search?” Mac asked sarcastically.

Jason looked at the slumped figures and nodded. “Might as well. Strictly speaking that can of beer was evidence.”

“The police can have the contents back in about an hour if they want,” said Mac as he stood up.

John had opened the rucksack and confirmed the timing devices were still in it. After a couple of minutes the three reappeared from upstairs and Ray advised Jason that explosives and detonators had been hidden in the loft behind the water storage tank but that there were no obvious booby traps. A total of three pistols had been discovered upstairs, which made four with the one on the kitchen floor. He had heard all of this through his earpiece as the search was carried out. Jason reckoned that would be enough to justify the killing of all eight terrorists. Along with the possibility that when the assault started the explosives could have been wired and ready to be set off, he didn't think anyone would object to a 'shoot to kill' approach. Hopefully Mac's three shots to the heads after the group in the lounge were killed would only be of academic interest to the coroner. He smiled to himself. It would be an easy enough job for the coroner this time. No signs of life; cause of death? Lead poisoning.

Jason radioed the police Bronze Command outside and confirmed that the house was secure, the explosives were there along with the remote detonators and four handguns. Bronze Command asked if any of the terrorists had been arrested and taken prisoner. Jason paused briefly before advising that none of them had been arrested and all of them were dead. He resisted the temptation to add, "Duh" but only just.

"We had to neutralise the threat that bombs were ready to go off at any time, you know that. Reading rights to armed terrorists as we went wasn't an option. Anyway the house and the bodies are ready for you to deal with, and as far as we can tell the explosive equipment is safe to handle."

He indicated to the figures inside that they were finished and clear to return to the van. Bob had joined them too, leaving only Sandy outside the house covering the front door. Jason told him over their radio net that they were leaving and Sandy indicated to the police teams outside that his team were about to come out of the house. They already knew from their own chain of command but seeing Sandy give a thumbs-up, take his mask off and light up reassured them too.

Chapter 44 - Bert Butterfield - and Closer

The following day, Bert made his way to the Social Services building in Dawn Harper's constituency. He had little in the way of a plan but knew if he could find Thelma Joyce he could at least get a story for the paper worth writing. If he could get an interview or uncover any dirt on her, or the family or find out the identity of Dawn's father then the story would run and run. Public interest seemed to justify whatever it took in his eyes.

The receptionist at Social Services was of an age that suggested she might not know Thelma as a work colleague, but Bert was pleasantly surprised to find out that she had met her briefly before her retirement. After a brief chat he also learned Thelma's address and that she too had never married. Sometimes this job was a bit too easy, Bert thought to himself. But then again, other times you had to work hard for every little break.

Bert decided this time that he would try phoning ahead to make an appointment; the doorstep approach was a bit intimidating for some and a bit too tabloid at times even for him. Thelma was in and seemed reassured that the phone call was from someone who knew Jean Miller well. Again, fortunately for Bert, Thelma was going to be in all day and could meet him that afternoon. Bert put the phone down and started doing a bit of background checking into the Joyce family. Like politicians, he always preferred to know the answer to the questions he asked if possible.

If Miss Miller was neat, tidy, obsessively clean and fit enough in retirement to play badminton five days a week, Thelma Joyce was the opposite in almost every respect. Bert found her dressed in shabby, frumpy clothes which barely disguised the fact that eating cream cakes was her only active sport. Her house looked like it hadn't been properly dusted or hoovered for years, which was in fact the case. The only thing they appeared to have in common was a sharp mind with excellent powers of recall.

Thelma had been put at ease by Bert's mention of Jean Miller but remained initially cautious when talking to him about Dawn Harper. After all, she had broken certain professional rules in following Dawn's life, after the initial adoption, and even more by attending school functions. Now retired, she wasn't as worried as she might have been whilst employed in Social Services, but a lifetime of adherence to principles designed to protect children’s well-being stayed with her.

"Hello, Mr Bronson," she said, showing Bert into her cat-dominated living room. "I'm not sure I should be talking to you at all, though."

Bert smiled, "Call me Bart, Thelma. I can assure you that Jean and I only discussed Dawn Harper in favourable terms and I do not intend to break any confidences in my book. After all it is focussed on the positive role models for girls in today's society, rather than on the life story of any one individual."

Bert could lie for Britain when he smelled a story.

"I'm happy to help you on that basis as long as you don't put any detail of Dawn's past in it which might hinder her career now."

"You don't need to worry on that score," assured Bert. "My intention is quite the opposite. I am just looking for some general background regarding Dawn's real family. Did you know her real mother, your cousin well?"

"Not hugely. We met up on family occasions like Christmas and some birthdays while we were all young but drifted apart as we got older. I kept in touch with Nicola's parents though. They were lovely, although they had lots of health problems later, even before Dawn was born."

"Was that why they didn't raise Dawn themselves, or did they not approve?"

Thelma raised an eyebrow of suspicion at this question but slowly corrected Bert.

"They loved Nicola and would have raised Dawn if they had been well enough to. They did take a great interest in the adoption process as far as they could."

"I assume Dawn's father was unable to help?" Bert asked in as guarded a way as he could. He didn't want the eyebrow to rise again and the flow of information to stop. He now knew that Dawn's real mother was Nicola Joyce and that she had been killed by a hit and run driver. It was already the bones of a news story. Any information about her father would be new ground completely; especially if he was still alive.

Thelma looked at Bert again. The eyebrow remained in its lower position and she continued.

"He hadn't been on the scene since conception I believe. Nicola had told her parents about him but he was apparently an explorer or mountaineer or some-such-thing. Either way he wasn't about. Whether he even knew he had become a father is doubtful. I visited Nicola in hospital after Dawn was born and the subject never arose. I felt we weren't close enough anymore for me to ask."

"I understand," reassured Bert. "I have cousins I haven't spoken to in years. At the occasional family funeral I hardly remember names anymore."

"You're right. Isn't it a shame?" said Thelma. "You play together when you're children almost like brothers and sisters but eventually lose touch so easily. That was part of the reason I kept an eye on Dawn later. I shouldn't have really but I felt somebody in the family should."

"I understand. Apart from her parents, were you the closest person to Nicola?"

"Not really. I was family but a friend of hers visited her at the same time in hospital when Dawn was born. I left early as I could tell Nicola was more comfortable talking to her. It was some friend from her job in politics - someone who had worked beside her when she was a researcher or whatever she did. The job had been her life during the election campaign, then all of a sudden she gave it up for the baby. Her parents were surprised, but then I suppose the maternal instinct is very strong. I never tested that out. I divided up my maternal instinct evenly amongst all the children I had to look after and came home each day glad to be out of it really."

"You don't remember the woman's name at all?"

"I do actually. She went on to become a local councillor here and ran unsuccessfully for parliament a couple of times. Her name is Jennifer Coombes. She is still a councillor here. I believe she and Dawn even worked together on women's issues within the council and at a national level on an all-party basis. I always liked that. I suspect Nicola would have approved too, although they are very much on opposite sides of the political fence."

Bert noted down the name Jennifer Coombes and her details, then pretended to note down other things that Thelma mentioned, but soon decided that she had mentioned everything he could make use of at this time. He already had enough to command part of the front page but his instinct suggested Jennifer Coombes might just be able shed some light on who Dawn's real father might have been. There was a good public interest angle on Dawn's mother being an activist for the other side. Dawn working with an unsuccessful candidate from the Tories on women's issues wasn't earth-shattering but the fact that this woman had been a friend of Nicola Joyce, Dawn's real mother, made it of interest. All he needed now was an angle on the father. A famous explorer or mountaineer would be good he thought, especially if he was still alive.

The following day Bert trawled through hundreds of articles on explorers, mountaineers and travel writers of any kind who might have been in Tory circles around the time Nicola became pregnant with Dawn. After eight hours solid and seven cups of coffee but no food, he gave up. No obvious candidate had leapt at him from the pages of the newspapers. He had found very few articles online about Nicola Joyce either and certainly none suggesting a liaison with any explorer. She was mentioned briefly in three ancient articles about the first successful election campaign of Sir Geoffrey Stanning where she appeared to have played a minor role. There were two reports of the hit and run accident which killed her in the local newspaper and that was it.

Further enquiries informed Bert of two key things. Firstly that Jennifer Coombes was a councillor of long-standing in Dawn's constituency, who represented one of the few Tory wards within its boundaries. Secondly he discovered that Jennifer was a lush. She appeared to have taken her early failure to win a seat at Westminster personally and had turned to the bottle in earnest after Dawn made the seat her own. There was little of this in the press beyond a brief report of her stumbling through a speech at a local school prize-giving. Thereafter she seemed to be accompanied by a minder from the party, according to Bert's contacts in the area, and rarely appeared in public after six at night or before ten in the morning. Bert resolved to try and gain access to her during her drinking hours. If he could have a chat as he plied her with drink it would be the best chance he had of finding out if she knew anything juicy regarding Dawn's past, particularly any information on her father.

It took Bert a few days to find out Jennifer's habits but he eventually found a window of opportunity. She tended to do her drinking at home, but the one exception was a monthly dinner and drinks with 'The Girls', as she called a group of close childhood friends she met with at a local hotel on these occasions. Bert's contact in the area suggested that the drink flowed freely and Jennifer usually had to be helped home by one of the husbands or a duty driver. Bert managed to find out the time and date of the next get-together and then set about hacking Jennifer's mobile phone.

Several days later Bert found himself parked in the car park of a very grand hotel which had at one time been somebody's even grander house. He watched a number of very affluent clients go in and out, including several women of a similar age to Jennifer Coombes, and was rewarded after half an hour or so when he saw her arrive too. He gave them a couple of hours to have a meal and chat before making his way inside to the bar nearest the restaurant. He had carried out a full reconnaissance two days earlier and knew his way about well. He also knew from Jennifer's phone conversations that she had arranged to stay on after the meal and drinks with one of her friends who presumably enjoyed a similar quantity of alcohol.

Bert ordered a drink and a light snack in the bar and waited for the group of women to finish their meal. He had to wait some time, as they obviously were in the habit of chatting at the table after the meal. Eventually they all came through together to the bar, although it was clear some of them were ready to leave, as they had their coats on and were saying their farewells. Once that element had left, Bert noticed only Jennifer and her friend from the phone call were left and they both ordered large glasses of red wine and sat on stools at the bar.

Bert finished his meal slowly and timed his arrival at the bar to coincide with the end of Jennifer's glass of wine. He smiled at her as he reached the bar and ordered a gin and tonic in as smooth a tone as he could. He also complimented the meal he had just eaten and left a generous tip as he paid for it.

Jennifer was fairly sozzled, as was her friend, but they had both noticed the well dressed younger man with the immaculate manners and Bert sensed one of them nudging the other with a playful wink as if to say, "He's a bit of all right".

Bert sat on a vacant barstool and sipped his gin and tonic. When he looked round at the ladies he caught Jennifer's eye and smiled again. It was enough of an excuse to start a conversation he decided.

"Excellent food here, isn't it?" he said, smiling again.

Jennifer and her friend agreed and they started making small talk. Bert offered them a drink which after initially declining they accepted. The evening then blossomed into a far more interesting one for the ladies than they had expected. The charming young man they had met who seemed to have no shortage of money or chat kept plying them with drink at his expense, and as the alcohol took its toll they began to wonder if he was in fact, attracted to one or both of them.

When Jennifer's friend excused herself and headed somewhat unsteadily to the ladies' toilets, Bert reached across and, placing his hand on her knee whispered, "Do you think your friend has had enough?"

Jennifer nodded agreement, no better herself but unaware of the fact. When her friend returned she suggested they called it a night. Her friend, who had been sick in the toilet, agreed and put her coat on, as did Jennifer. They headed for the door, but not before Jennifer and Bert had exchanged winks.

Having seen her friend into a taxi, Jennifer returned to the bar and took her coat off. Bert ordered yet another drink and started to really pile on the charm. As a mere executive in retail banking his life was dull compared to that of a local councillor and successful business woman.

Jennifer was hooked and started on her well rehearsed complaints about not being elected to parliament due to dirty tricks on the part of jealous opposition candidates etc. etc.

Bert managed to keep the conversation on politics and mentioned how impressed he was with the local Member of Parliament, Dawn Harper, who he had to acknowledge was a great debater despite not sharing his politics.

Jennifer leaned forward and whispered, "I knew her mother. She was one of us, though."

"And her father too no doubt?" Bert added casually.

Jennifer looked around cautiously, nearly falling off her stool in the process. Bert steadied her with one hand on her shoulder and another dangerously high on her leg. Then Jennifer leaned forward.

"Nobody knows this, and it must go no further," She slurred.

Bert made a sign to suggest that his lips were sealed and leaned forward placing his hand on her knee again.

"Her father was... is one of us," said Jennifer with a wink.

"Thought so," nodded Bert as if he wasn't interested in any further details. "Local guy?"

Jennifer leaned forward and placed her hand on Bert's knee closer to his crotch than he had expected.

"Geoff Stanning," said Jennifer and sat back.

Bert missed the significance for a second until his brain registered the name with his recent research on Nicola Joyce.

"The politician? Sir Geoffrey Stanning?" he asked in genuine disbelief.

Jennifer nodded and touched the side of her nose to emphasise that it was their little secret.

"Not for fucking long it won't be," thought Bert as his brain started thinking through all the possible headlines which this story conjured up.

"My lips are sealed," lied Bert before adding, "As are Sir Geoffrey's, no doubt."

"He doesn't know," whispered Jennifer with a schoolgirl giggle which looked somehow ridiculous on her middle aged face. "Of course he knew he fathered a child with Nicola, but nothing after that. Nicola told me in confidence when Dawn was born. Nobody else knows what happened to the child afterwards. Geoff never knew and Dawn doesn't know, so it's important we keep schtum."

"Mum's the word," said Bert.

"Or dad's the word in this case," he thought to himself.

Jennifer ordered another round of drinks and excused herself before making unsteady progress towards the ladies'.

When she eventually returned the charming young man was nowhere to be seen and she staggered off to get a taxi, disappointed and vaguely aware she may have been a trifle indiscreet.

When Bert got home he checked that he had the conversation clearly on tape from his hidden microphone and was relieved to find it was as clear as day. Jennifer Coombes, failed parliamentary candidate and long serving Tory councillor, admits that Dawn Harper, Labour's Shadow Families Minister, was in fact the secret love child of the Prime Minister's Parliamentary Private Secretary.

You couldn't make it up, he thought. At least he couldn't have made it up. Fortunately for him though, and thanks to Jennifer Coombes, he didn't have to. He could retire on the strength of this one.

The phone calls on Jennifer Coombes' mobile phone also yielded some gold-dust for Bert Butterfield. There were a few business-like calls the day after Bert had met her at the hotel but the following day there was a call to somebody in Central Office. Jennifer had obviously been wrestling with her conscience regarding giving away secrets to a complete stranger in a hotel, whilst drunk. Had she considered for a moment that the stranger was an investigative reporter who had also tapped into her personal phone calls she would have felt a lot worse. As it was she phoned to ask if she could have a private meeting with Sir Geoffrey Stanning as soon as it could be arranged. When she was turned down she tried again mentioning that it was on an extremely delicate matter and it was therefore vital that she met with Sir Geoffrey soon and alone. No, she couldn't leave a message or discuss the matter with anyone else. Again she was turned down by return call.

When she mentioned that it was regarding the late Nicola Joyce the answer came back quite differently. Sir Geoffrey could fit in a brief meeting with her, and first thing the following day happened to suit him. The Palace of Westminster wouldn't be suitable so they would meet for lunch at a private club. Jennifer was clearly relieved. Bert was ecstatic. He arranged for a photographer to take pictures of both parties arriving at the club and to note down the people, date and time for later verification. Bert provided no other details to any of his colleagues at this time.

Over the course of the next 24 hours Bert was able to monitor calls from Sir Geoffrey's aides to Jennifer and, after their meeting, he hit pay-dirt with a late night call from a shattered Sir Geoffrey to Jennifer. Although he could never use it legally, he taped the call to ensure he had any details discussed correctly. Then he sat down to finish his front page piece before phoning his editor and telling him to keep the front page clear the following day for the story of the decade. His editor tried to get a hint of the gist of it but Bert wouldn't waiver.

"I'll be there first thing in the morning with all the details and a story ready to go. You'll love it, trust me," and with that he hung up and poured himself a large whisky straight from a bottle on his desk. "Oh yes !" he thought to himself. "You've still got it."

Chapter 45 - Best Served Hot

After Jennifer Coombes left Sir Geoffrey's office, he sat down in his seat in shock. He had just managed to maintain his composure as he listened to her lay out the bombshell about to hit his career. To begin with, he could not believe what she was telling him, and then couldn't believe that after keeping the secret for so long she had blurted it out to a complete stranger. He was sure right away that the man had been a reporter, and after less than twenty minutes online Jennifer was able to confirm for him that the 'salesman' had been none other than Bert Butterfield, the most tabloid of tabloid hacks.

He managed to thank her for letting him know before it became public but collapsed with his head in his hands the moment she left his office.

The fact that he had had an affair, brief as it was, would be enough to finish him off and ruin his 'legacy' of public service. Many might be sympathetic in his constituency if that had been the whole story. Instead he would become a laughing stock in the press and a liability to his party. He had fathered and then ignored an illegitimate daughter who suffered greatly as a result of being orphaned and abandoned, but still rose to prominence in the very opposition which was endangering a further term in office for his boss, the Prime Minister.

It was a moment or two before he then realised that his wife might be a tad upset too. Their happy family life had been based on something of a lie if he had slept with one of his campaign team thirty years before. He thought it unlikely she would actually walk out; they were too old for that drama, but he would have some tough explaining to do and his home life would be a misery from that day forward. Rightly so, he thought as he pictured Nicola again as she had been when he saw her last. He tried to think of Dawn Harper as a poor, defenceless waif, but that image was impossible to conjure up. What she would make of it he had no idea: It was unlikely she would add him to her Christmas card list and call him Daddy on the phone. His politician's mind tried to figure out if it would play to her advantage or not. He couldn't decide. He knew, however, that he was stuffed whatever happened.

As he thought it through he couldn't dispel the image of Nicola's body on a pavement, killed and left to die like road kill. He found himself blaming Sir Crispin, even though he hadn't been involved. It was, however, somebody of his like who had carried out the action to silence her. It had been the Prime Minister's father.

Normally a man completely in control of his emotions Sir Geoffrey found rage welling up within him.

If this was the end for him he was going to take as many of the bastards with him as he could. If he could get hold of Sir Crispin's notebook and at least some of the associated files he could create a whirlwind of publicity which would make his infidelity look like trivia. He found himself formulating a plan of action, a plan of pure, undiluted revenge, and he would have to put it into action before it was too late and he was excluded from the circle of power for ever.

Sir Geoffrey phoned Sir Crispin's office and was pleased to find him in.

"Crispin? I need another look at that chart of yours if that's okay; just so that I can fully brief the PM."

"Certainly," agreed the Chief Whip, a little surprised that his colleague hadn't fully noted the identity of the rebels at their recent meeting. "Now?"

"If at all possible. Sorry to be a pest."

"Head down now and I'll leave you to it. I have a meeting shortly, so you can have peace to get the picture clear. Just lock the door behind you when you leave as I might be a while and don't want any prying eyes on the list."

Sir Crispin was on route to a rather particular social gathering which he knew would go on well into the evening. He had waited for this get-together with eager anticipation and was not about to let anyone delay his departure. The event might not be quite up to the ones he had enjoyed in the good old days at Dolphin Square but it was as close as anyone dared to arrange these days and he couldn't wait.

"Will do, old boy," confirmed Sir Geoffrey before heading off to Crispin's office.

Sir Crispin never batted an eyelid as his Sir Geoffrey arrived, his mind clearly on other things.

"Remember to pull the door behind you when you're finished, there's a good chap," and with that Sir Geoffrey found himself alone in the Chief Whip's private office. He looked around and found that Sir Crispin had again left his briefcase in the office. He guessed it had never crossed his colleague's mind that it wouldn't be safe if left there.

He closed the door and took the precaution this time of locking it on the inside to buy himself time if needs be; he planned to get as much information as possible on this occasion before leaving and didn't want to be stopped in the process.

He opened the briefcase and took out the diary again. He worked his way through a few prominent members of the cabinet, jotting down the file references in a shorthand notebook he had brought with him for the purpose. Then he looked round the room. He was sure that Sir Crispin wouldn't risk having the detailed files anywhere else but here in his office. Security throughout the building was tight and should anything befall Sir Crispin the files would simply pass to his successor to use as he saw fit. There were a number of standard filing cabinets in the room which he quickly ascertained held nothing of any great interest to him in his present search. Another detailed look revealed a large fireguard against one wall which he must have seen a thousand times before without taking note of it. On closer inspection he discovered that it was being used to hide a small, two-drawer filing cabinet which he noticed did not have a key in it, unlike the others.

"Bingo," he thought to himself.

He took a large, flat-head screw driver from inside his jacket and whispered to himself, " In for a penny: In for a pound."

He forced the screwdriver into the top of the cabinet hoping it would ping open quite easily. It didn't the first time, but if he had acquired anything in politics it was weight. He forced the screwdriver further in and leaned his entire bulk onto it. The drawer bent at the top before the lock gave up the unequal struggle and opened slightly. He put the screwdriver down and looked at the damage he had done. It was too late now to back out. He pulled open the drawer and looked in. To his relief inside were files in neat hanging folders and he immediately recognised the references as matching those in Sir Crispin's notebook.

Working fast he checked some of the people he had picked out earlier. The list contained a few high profile names with secrets which were particularly embarrassing and, in two cases, highly illegal. He quickly opened the first file, intending merely to check it verified what the notebook had suggested but couldn't believe the details he had started reading. After a few minutes he managed to tear himself away and quickly checked the other files he had selected.

Once he had them all, he had a sudden thought. Leafing through the notebook he turned to see if the Prime Minister was listed. When he found the entry he couldn't believe what he found. The details appeared to relate mainly to the period before the PM became an MP but there were dates after that too and the file contained information of activities Sir Geoffrey couldn't initially picture his boss engaged in. He started rifling through the cabinet until he found the relevant file and found it, neatly in its place. Inside were details of locations, dates and individuals which made the colour drain from his face as he read. How on earth had he been unaware of this? From the file it was clear that others within the party must have known and indeed been involved. Even to an insider like Geoffrey it was all a shock. It was also the best insurance policy he could think of having in place when the newspapers were about to expose his affair and fathering of the Harpie. His little secret wouldn't even make page five of the papers on the same day as the PM's past became public.

He looked round but realised he hadn't brought a briefcase with him and carrying these particular files to his own office and eventually home wouldn't be wise. After a moment's pause he decided "to hell with it" and shoved the files into Sir Crispin's briefcase. Might as well be hung for a sheep as a lamb he thought. Then he kicked the cabinet shut, and pocketed the screwdriver. He carefully unlocked the door and looked out. The corridor outside was empty. He quickly left the office and pulled the door locked shut behind him.

He was about to walk away when he had a sudden flash of inspiration. He looked around and found the coast still clear. With a brief run and massive shove with his shoulder he forced the door open again, breaking the frame and rendering the lock useless. The corridor was still clear. He hurried away from the scene of the crime, checking his watch as he went.

"That might delay things slightly," he thought to himself. "A little bit of plausible deniability."

Chapter 46 - Sue in Danger

The day after the troops had left, Sue found herself struggling to cope with the workload of the twins on her own. She had managed it fine before they arrived at the safe house but had become used to an enormous amount of help in recent weeks. The routine of feeding, nappy changing and everything else had been spread over a large group of willing hands and she missed them enormously now they had gone. She even missed Mac.

Once the twins were fed, changed and dressed she decided to take them out and do some shopping as she had done with Sandy so often recently. She didn't actually need anything in particular but felt trapped and alone. She desperately wanted to see people and speak to them.

She carefully put the boys into their buggy and took some of the money the men had left with her, hiding the rest under the mattress of her bed, then headed out to the street. It was a fairly mild day and she took in deep breaths of fresh air. Slowly her mood lifted and she felt a little bit more positive about the future. One thing she had to do, though, was phone Brian as soon as she got back and make sure he was sorting something out for her on a more permanent basis. Since she had delivered her ultimatum she had heard nothing from him or David and was hoping it meant he was busy making arrangements for them, but she couldn't leave it to chance.

Later she couldn't remember exactly when she became aware of the van behind her in the street. It could have pulled out from a parking space somewhere near the house, but if it had she hadn't noticed it at the time. As she reached the corner of the road, however, she sensed it was following her at a walking pace. The realisation gave her a start. She looked round, hoping it was some of Jason's guys keeping an eye on her but the face at the wheel was that of a stranger. When he saw her turn and look directly at him he immediately gunned the engine and aimed the unmarked transit van straight at her and the pram. She screamed and looked round for cover or anyone who could help, but the street was empty of people and cars.

At the last moment, before the van reached her, Sue's life seemed to slow down and she was able to think clearly through her options almost in slow motion. She saw a gap between cars at the other side of the road and managed to push the pram with all the force she could muster towards it. At the same time she threw herself backwards into a narrow doorway behind her. The van crashed past her, scraping the wall as it went, and the wing mirror caught her hard on the shoulder.

The van screeched to a halt as quickly as it could after the doorway, but far enough past it to allow Sue to rush out and cross the street towards the pram and the twins, who were both now howling in fright. She ran across to the pram and grabbed it, turning in terror to see the van reversing towards the gap between the cars. She managed to push herself and the twins behind the shelter of one of cars as the van smashed into the other one and the wall beside the pavement. As she started to push the pram along the pavement at a run, she saw the driver wrestle with the gears and start pursuing her along the street. She kept looking back and could make out an overweight but powerful-looking figure behind the wheel. He had a look of grim determination on his face and was cursing as he drove.

Another white van appeared, coming along the street the opposite way and both drivers saw each other just in time to avoid a head on collision. They swerved and just clipped each other. The van which had been trying to ram Sue and the boys straightened after swerving before the driver decided to give up his attack and sped off into the distance.

The other van stopped with a screech of brakes and for a second Sue panicked that it was driven by an accomplice of the first attacker. Instead, when the driver got out of the cab she was relieved to see it was the Sikh man who owned the convenience store nearest to the safe house. He stared at the dent in his van, quite oblivious to the danger Sue had just survived.

"What a bloody lunatic," he shouted. "He could have killed somebody driving like that. Did you get his number?"

Sue shook her head before realising that her whole body was shaking too.

"I'm afraid not," she said, before adding automatically, "Are you okay?"

"I'm fine," said the shopkeeper, "But this bloody van is almost new. If I get my hands on him I'll..."

The sentence wasn't finished as he realised it would never happen and as he had never so much as been in fight in the school playground he was unlikely to start and win one now. Aside from that, he realised he was speaking to one of his best customers and didn't want to scare her off. Instead he just smiled, shrugged his shoulders and got back into his van and drove off, leaving Sue alone once more.

By now there were some other people walking along the street and a few cars who had stopped to see why a van was stopped almost sideways in the street. Sue took confidence in their presence and headed quickly back to the house. She opened the door and dragged the pram in as swiftly as she could, locking the door securely behind her. Then she searched the whole house to make sure nobody was there before collapsing on the sofa with a child in each arm to comfort them.

"What the hell was that all about?" she wondered to herself. She wondered for a second if the troops had been ordered to get rid of her in case she told somebody of their whereabouts, but immediately dismissed the thought. None of the guys would have been a party to what had just happened. Even if they had wanted to get rid of her they could have done it more easily at some point while living there. No, it wasn't Jason's guys, she was sure of that. If not them, then who? Who would want to kill her and the twins? A slow realisation dawned in her mind. Brian bloody Smithe and his cronies, that's who. With the realisation came fear. If he had given up on her and had powerful friends who could organise an attack on her like the one which she had just narrowly escaped from, then she was in deep trouble. She felt suddenly more alone than she had ever felt in her life, and that was saying something. Whoever was after her would try again until they were successful. She found herself crying and hated herself for it but couldn't stop. She reached into the pocket of her jeans for a tissue to dry the tears. She needed to think. She needed a plan. She needed help, but if Brian had washed his hands of her she couldn't hope for any help from any of her former colleagues. As she pulled the tissue from her pocket a folded page from a small pocket notebook fell out. She opened it and read the remarkably neat writing on one side.

"John Stanley", followed by a mobile number.

Chapter 47 - John the Beast's Last Day

Jason sat at his desk the day after the raid, completing paperwork and looking forward to a week's leave. He was also looking forward to the prospect of returning as a newly promoted Squadron Commander and liked the idea of the new role. Unfortunately it was unlikely he would be able to take part in as much, if any, front line activities now. In consolation he had taken an important step on the promotion ladder without having to leave the Regiment, so it wasn't all bad. A mention in despatches for the recent work in London would do no harm in the long term either. All in all; life was good.

His diary had a number of entries in it for the day but not enough to tie him to the desk beyond the morning; another good thing. The first item was a strange one though, written in The RSM's unmistakable scrawl: "Formal interview request from L/Cpl John Stanley (John the Beast)."

At the appointed hour there was a knock on his office door.

"Come in," he shouted.

The door opened and John the Beast marched in wearing barrack dress. He crashed to a halt and saluted, all of which was most unusual.

"At ease John, for fuck sake," said Jason. "What's going on?"

"I'm leaving boss."

"What do you mean you're leaving? The Regiment?"

"No Boss, The Army. I've decided it's not for me. I've made other plans."

Jason looked at the soldier standing in front of him and half expected him to laugh and say it was all a joke, but that didn't happen.

"What do you mean, it's not for you?" he began, trying to make sense of the situation. "You've been a soldier for seventeen years, twelve of those with the Regiment. You have a Military Medal, two Mentions in Dispatches and four CO's commendations to your name. That suggests you're pretty good at the job. For fuck's sake, if the army isn't for you, who the hell is it for?"

"I plan to enrol on a social work course in London. Counselling teenagers basically. I think I'll be good at it. Straighten some of the wilder ones out before they really go off the rails. I've already done the first year's work by distant learning." After a pause he continued, "I want to resign with immediate effect and head to London today. Not sure what paperwork you need but I'll sign it, whatever it is."

"Have you any idea what you are doing, man? It's not straightforward to adjust to Civvy Street after this lark. Have you even sorted out a place to live? That's neither easy nor cheap in London and there won't be much of a payoff if you leave right now."

"I've sorted that boss. I'm moving in with Sue."

"Who?" asked Jason, aware that John was unmarried and had never mentioned a steady girlfriend. Then the penny dropped. "Susan White?"

"Yes, Boss, she phoned me last night and she's asked me to move in. She needs help with the kids and I'll be there if anyone else tries to harm them. She had a bit of a scare yesterday and I know it's not the first time she has been under threat. She is terrified for her life and the twins. Thinks she knows who's behind it too."

"Well I'll be buggered! You are a dark horse John. Are you one hundred per cent sure about this?"

John stared him straight in the eyes and confirmed he was. All doubt was removed from Jason's mind.

“Okay, pack your things. I’ll sort the paperwork and we’ll get it signed sometime. For now you’re on leave. I’ll keep the pay going as long as I can. Good luck. You’ll need it one way or another.”

At that Jason stood up and shook hands with the giant soldier standing in front of his desk. After that, John saluted, about turned and marched out of the office and the army.

Jason waited for a few minutes then picked up his phone. Dialling an internal number he waited till the call was answered.

“RSM, John the Beast’s on indefinite leave for now, domestic problems... No I didn’t know he had any domestic arrangements either, but he does. I’ll keep you posted.”

The voice at the other end confirmed he had got the message and the call ended.

Jason stared out of his office window. "God help anyone who tries to harm that little family group," he thought to himself. "And God help any teenage trouble makers who didn’t take John’s advice about mending their ways."

Chapter 48 – The Press

Sue sat in the safe house, wondering what to do next. She was certain now that Brian had ordered her dead, or at least been aware of others organising that on his behalf. John had explained that had it not been for him and Mac she would no doubt be dead already, along with her children. She desperately wanted revenge; to bring that bastard down along with anyone else who had been involved. The problem was how to do it and keep herself and the boys safe. To her surprise John had insisted that he came back to the house as soon as he could, assuring her that meant today. He might not have Jason's looks but for now he was the man of her dreams. There was also the little matter of making sure the lads who had saved her from Jack Hunter didn't end up going to jail for killing him.

The television was on in the background and she watched as each report from home and abroad played out and looked at the politicians being interviewed, wondering which ones might have been aware of Brian's plan, if indeed he had been the orchestrator.

One interview in particular, caught her eye.

The Shadow Minister for Families, Dawn Harper, was being interviewed about government plans to cut benefits to lone parents and was furiously denouncing the changes which, she said, vilified some of the most vulnerable members of society and condemned their children to poverty. The government was doing this whilst allowing the wealthy elite to avoid millions in tax as a matter of course.

"Single mothers don't live in poverty as a lifestyle choice," she said as she finished.

"You can say that again," echoed Sue.

The report then switched to Brian Smithe outside The Houses of Parliament, who re-affirmed the Government position that single mothers had a choice in having children in most cases and shouldn't expect to be bailed out by the hard working tax-payer.

Sue's blood boiled as she watched and her mind was suddenly made up.

If she could speak to Dawn Harper and let her know that the Minister for Families was denouncing single mothers despite fathering twins with his former researcher he would be finished for certain. If that didn't give her the ammunition to destroy Brian's career nothing would. The simple fact of his utter lack of integrity would finish him off without having to supply any details of her recent house guests and the late unlamented Jack Hunter.

Chapter 49 – A Busy Night Ahead

Sir Crispin Jessop took a tube to the station-but-one nearest to Dudley's and walked the rest of the way. He was glad that it was raining heavily and he could turn the collar of his coat up. He also carried an umbrella which hid his identity still further. He had no real fear of anyone watching his movements but he had no great desire to be recognised either. All in all, a murky, rainy night was ideal. It also matched both his mood and the dark nature of his intentions. He took the lane to the rear of the club and arrived at the staff entrance. He knocked quickly and was immediately shown in by one of the oldest and longest serving members of staff. Gavin took Sir Crispin's coat and umbrella without any fuss or acknowledgement, conscious of the fact that a member arriving at the staff door of Dudley's did so for reasons of confidentiality. In other words; they were not there.

Without a word Sir Crispin made his way to a small private dining room close to the rear of the premises which was used on occasions when privacy was essential. There he found Mr Smith and Mr Brown already seated along with another man. He nodded as he entered the room and looked at the men in turn, focusing briefly on their eyes to calculate their resolve and loyalty.

“A series of telephone calls to journalists and others tonight has potentially placed a number of people and previous activities by yourselves into the spotlight. As a result I have had to call you all together here at short notice to brief you personally on what is required. Suffice to say you are all in for a very busy night!”

With that he handed each man an envelope which contained simple instructions and the names of those who their targets were this time. A few eyebrows were raised as the men read the details but none of them spoke. This evening would be about self-preservation as much as anything else and they knew it. Despite his emotionless expression, Mr Smith was surprised to notice that the first of his tasks was located in Dudley's itself.

"Oh well," he thought to himself. "Saves going out in the rain just yet."

Chapter 50 - Back at the House

As soon as he left Jason's office, L/Cpl John Stanley, late of the Special Air Service, almost ran to his billet and changed into his civvy clothes and out of uniform for the last time.

As he was doing so Mac came into the room, fully aware of his colleague's intentions.

"I made up some sandwiches for the trip," he said, handing John a brown paper bag of the type usually used for packed lunches.

From the weight of it John knew straight away that it contained Jack Hunter's gun.

"Being a thieving Jock bastard, I went through that guy's pockets and his car and found this too," said Mac, handing over an envelope of cash he had found in the glove compartment of Jack's car.

John looked at him and nodded. "Thanks, mate."

Then the two shook hands and John grabbed his rucksack and left.

He drove as fast as he could from Hereford to London but not so fast as to draw attention from any police cars on the M4. He arrived at the safe house late in the afternoon and parked his car as near to the door as he could before jogging over and ringing the doorbell.

Inside the house Sue had been sitting with the twins trying to keep herself busy and not dwell on her recent experience with the unknown assailant. John the Beast had promised he would get there as soon as possible but she guessed that would take some time. When the doorbell rang she jumped in fear. The twins seemed to sense this and started crying. She lifted the rockers they were in and put them out of sight in the kitchen quickly before cautiously making her way to the front door as the bell rang again.

"Who is it?" she asked in a trembling voice.

"John Stanley," came the reply.

Momentarily confused by her fear she asked, "Who?"

There was a sigh outside the door and pause before a reluctant voice said, "John the Beast."

Sue opened the door and John slipped quickly into the house, locking the door behind him as he did so.

Sue looked at the huge figure who had answered her cry for help and grabbed him round the waist, bursting into tears as she did so. He let her hug her for a few minutes till she calmed down and then directed her through to the lounge with a surprisingly gentle arm around her shoulder.

"You're safe now," he said. "I won't let anybody hurt you or the twins ever again."

Chapter 51 - Goodbye to Dudley's

Sir Geoffrey sat in his room in Dudley's reading through the files he had taken from Sir Crispin's office. The details were beyond anything he could have dreamed up about some of his colleagues. He knew that if it became known that he had the files he would be in great danger. He had made four copies of each of several key documents before making for the club and now put these into a large envelope. He wrote the address of the London office of a German tabloid newspaper on the front, for the attention of a specific journalist he knew and disliked. He addressed another to The Guardian, one to his wife, the final one to Bert Butterfield. Once they were ready he rang the bell to call for a member of staff and was relieved to see Gavin, Dudley's most senior and trusted porter arrive.

"Gavin, please see that these envelopes are couriered immediately. They are important government matters and must catch the last collection today."

Gavin nodded, taking his task very seriously. His job involved the trust of ministers, judges, generals and business leaders who relied on him for all manner of services. If Sir Geoffrey Stanning wanted these couriered immediately they must be important, and he would see to it personally before anything else diverted his attention.

As he walked out of the lift on the ground floor he was passed by one of the men he had let in through the staff door for the meeting with Sir Crispin Jessop. It was curious, as the man was definitely not a member. He shrugged his shoulders and continued with his task.

Chapter 52 - Bert Butterfield - Gotcha !

Bert sat in his flat, having typed and proof-read his article regarding Sir Geoffrey's secret love-child. He loved it. He had also worked out the structure of several follow-up articles. It would knock both the main parties for six, which he regarded as the icing on the cake. The great and the good were always legitimate targets for him, and the fact that Dawn Harper seemed to be a fairly genuine person focused on doing good was lost on him. He saved a copy of the article and supporting interview transcripts onto a flash-drive and hid it in the usual place, where only his closest friend, his lawyer and his editor could find it.

He poured himself a drink and decided that he would celebrate the scoop by going out for dinner and washing it down with some very expensive wine. He would even send the bill to his editor. Bert knew he would pay anything once he saw the story in the morning. He would pay for any meal, any wine, a car, even a bloody yacht if Bert asked him, such was the nature of the story.

He grabbed his jacket and headed out, making for an expensive restaurant he knew nearby. This time he wouldn't take a taxi; he would walk. He needed some fresh air to clear his head and give him an appetite.

As he walked down his own street he failed to see the white transit van pull out of a space a hundred yards behind him, so wrapped up was he in his latest success. At the wheel was a large, overweight man with a grim look on his face. He had failed once recently and it had been made quite clear to him that further failure would not be tolerated. From the look of Bert's casual progress along the pavement, this job would be a piece of cake. After that he had to collect Bert's computer and a hidden flash drive before making good his mistake from the previous day. Once he had done that he had to deliver the computer equipment to an address he had dropped things off at before. His employer had been right; it would be a busy night.

Chapter 53 - Two for the Price of One

Mr Brown watched Dawn Harper leave her flat and was disappointed to see her run quickly into the waiting taxi, giving him no opportunity to carry out his instructions.

"Never mind," he thought to himself, "If I follow her all night I'll get another chance, one way or another. Once he had taken care of her he could focus on the second target for the night. He had to meet the rest of the team and ensure that the woman with the twins was silenced for good. Whether Jack Hunter had chickened out of his task or something had gone wrong as he tried to complete it was now irrelevant. A second botched attempt had not gone down well with the powers-that-be and Brown had instructions to help Smith deal with the person responsible as soon as all other matters had been resolved. Neither Smith nor Brown had been entirely convinced that Jack Hunter or their overweight ex-army colleague were suitable for wet work and events had proved them right.

He followed the taxi preparing himself for what was to come. As it made its way through London, Brown found himself recognising the route from his earlier checks on a street plan of the capital. Slowly but surely it made its way through the evening traffic to the address in Cricklewood where he was expecting to go much later on. The taxi stopped near the front door of Sue's house and Dawn Harper quickly paid and sprinted to the door which opened immediately to let her in.

Mr Brown raised his eyebrow in surprise. This was an unexpected turn of events but could make things a whole lot easier: two for the price of one.

Chapter 54 - The Birthday Girls

Dawn found that the door to the house opened as soon as she arrived and got the fright of her life as she found herself staring at a huge man behind the door instead of Susan White. Seeing the look of fear on her face John smiled to reassure her, a gesture which rarely worked.

"Sue's through there with the twins," he said, pointing towards the lounge as he locked the front door again.

Dawn walked into the lounge and found Sue White sitting watching TV with one twin in her arms and the other asleep in a rocker at her feet.

"I'm Dawn Harper. I came as fast as I could when I got your message. It seems we share a common loathing of the Minister for Families? By the way, who's the big guy in the hallway?"

Sue shook the hand that was offered to her and smiled.

"He's my guardian angel," Sue chuckled.

"You must be the safest woman in London," Dawn added, joining in the nervous laughter.

After cups of tea had been made, Sue slowly but surely told Dawn everything which had happened to her during the time working as a researcher for Brian Smithe. She even apologised for keeping Dawn's birthday flowers. Dawn had started by taking notes, but after a while stopped and just listened to the story as it unfolded. Very quickly she realised Brian's political career was finished with immediate effect. The only question was how and when to make the revelations public. One of the main considerations as far as that was concerned was Sue's safety. While the two women were talking, John walked through the lounge and into the kitchen to make himself a mug of tea and Dawn decided that for the moment Sue's personal safety was actually fine.

Chapter 55 - White Van Men

Mr Brown sat in the Range Rover within view of the house where Dawn had apparently arrived to meet the mother of the twins, and sent a couple of text messages to numbers he had been given in Dudley's using an unregistered phone which he had bought for the purpose. About an hour later, Mr Smith arrived with the chubby colleague they were calling Mr Green in an unmarked white transit van. As soon as they arrived they walked quickly and calmly to the Range Rover and got into the back seats.

"We have recovered the files from Dudley's, the computer and the flash drive from the hack. They're locked in the back of the van," said Mr White

Mr Brown nodded at his colleague with a knowing look but said nothing to Mr Green who sat in the back of the vehicle sweating profusely.

After a further short discussion Mr Green left the vehicle carrying a tool box which he had brought from the van and made his way towards the back of the house. After a pause Mr Smith walked slowly to the front door of the house and checked his watch.

Chapter 56 - An end to the Bullies

Meanwhile in the kitchen John made himself a brew and looked round. There was very little food in the house now and he knew that sooner or later he would have to get some himself from the nearby shop or make a trip together with sue and the twins.

When the noise of the kettle stopped he just heard a noise from the back yard of the house: a noise which sounded like a gate being forced and somebody breathing heavily. It was faint from inside the building but unmistakably human and now close outside.

John moved swiftly to the back door and unlocked it, keen to avoid any further noise which might attract the attention of the women next door. He hid out of sight in a cupboard beyond the back door away from the kitchen from where he could still see the door handle. After a minute or two he saw the handle turn and the door start to open slowly. The breathing was still just audible, which allowed him to gauge where the man was and to time his attack just right.

John knocked the man out cold and dragged the unconscious body outside to an old wash-house, gagging and trussing the man up first. He pocketed the pistol the man had been carrying and returned quickly to the kitchen, securing the door behind him. Just as he was trying to figure out what to do next, Sue appeared from the lounge in a panic.

"There's somebody picking the lock on the front door."

"Shit," thought John to himself. "What next?"

He raced through the lounge at a speed which bellied his massive frame, indicating to Dawn as he passed that she should stay there whatever happened next.

He made it to the hall just as the front door opened and with no alternative charged the door and the bulky figure behind it simultaneously. There was a groan and a crashing fall, which in most cases would have suggested that a person had ceased to be a threat, but Smith was up and turning with his gun in his hand by the time John had slammed the door shut to see who had broken in.

Smith managed to loose off one quick shot which caught John in the right hand side of his chest, near the shoulder, before the gun was viciously kicked from his hand and his world collapsed into a painful and dark place.

Outside Mr Brown heard the shot and knew something had gone badly wrong inside. Green had a silencer on his weapon and the plan involved him using that to kill the occupants of the house. If a gun had been fired then it was either Smith or somebody else inside, and neither option was good. He jumped out of the Range Rover and walked quickly over to the house. He would have to move quickly to finish the job and get clear in case somebody alerted the police. With that in mind, he pulled the gun from his pocket and opened the door in one swift movement.

When Smith had stopped moving, John rolled over to examine his wound. It was deep, painful and was bleeding badly. He propped himself up against the wall and knew that he would need medical attention quickly or he would almost certainly pass out. He had dropped his gun when he was hit and started edging towards it, still unsure what to do next.

Before he could get to the gun, though, the front door opened and another bulky figure burst in holding a gun. The figure looked at Smith's body lying just inside the door and then at John who was trying to get to the fallen gun. The figure looked down at John and kicked his gun away before picking up Smith's gun and putting it into his pocket.

"So that explains what happened," he said, keeping his gun pointed at John all the time.

Brown was just about to say something else when his head seemed to explode and John was immediately covered in blood. There had been no sound, and John wondered if he had somehow been the one who had been shot and this was the confusion of the senses which came with death. Then he watched as the figure in the door way fell forward on top of the other body.

A few seconds later the unmistakable scrawny features of Mac popped into view.

"Hi, big guy. I knew you would need a hand."

"I never, ever thought I would be pleased to see your face, you ugly Jock bastard, but I am," John managed to say.

Mac bent over and covered John's wound with a jumper which he had been carrying to conceal his silenced pistol. He pressed hard and John fainted for a few minutes. When he came to, Mac was beside him again, but both bodies had miraculously disappeared.

Mac had that infuriating grin on his face which annoyed everyone who worked with him, but John could have kissed it this time. Well, almost.

"Look what I found in their van," said Mac holding a pile of files, a computer and a flash drive in his hand. "I had a quick look in one of the files which had that wanker Pearson's name on it and you wouldn't believe what he's been up to. Not quite sure what to do with it, but we need to get the fuck out of here quickly."

"Leave it for Sue and her friend next door. They'll make very good use of it, trust me."

Mac looked sceptical for a second but accepted the advice and started helping his friend up. They made their way outside to where Mac had parked the white van near the front door. With a struggle, John made it into the passenger seat and Mac jumped in the driver's side.

"Just drop me at the nearest A&E then leg it and get rid of the bodies," said John before adding. "That reminds me, there's another one in the back yard who is not quite as dead as these two."

"Fuck sake," said Mac. "You had to make a meal of it didn't you? We'll get him on the way round."

John watched from the van, drifting in and out of consciousness, as Mac struggled with the now very recently deceased body of Mr Green and finally got it into the back of the van with the other two.

As the van drove away with a squeal of tyres John turned to his friend, feeling it might be his last lucid moment for a while.

"Thanks mate, but I thought you were heading back to Glasgow on leave?"

Mac turned towards him with a shrug.

"I decided not to go home this time. Four kids is enough for anyone."

Chapter 57 - End of the Beginning - Beginning of the End

In the lounge of the safe house, Dawn and Sue strained their ears to make out what was happening in the hall way. When they heard a shot they instinctively grabbed each other before turning to the twins, taking one each in their arms and running to the kitchen. Sue then took both of the boys while Dawn looked round for any form of weapon.

"What the fuck is going on?" she whispered to Sue.

"Whoever tried to kill me before must have come back for another go," replied Sue under her breath as Dawn took the largest kitchen knife she could find out of the drawer and held it tight, ready in case somebody other than John came through the kitchen door.

They stood like that for fifteen minutes but nothing happened. Eventually Dawn indicated that she was going to have a look. Sue tried to stop her but Dawn headed through to the lounge anyway. The room was exactly as they had left it. There was no noise coming from the hall so she cautiously approached the doorway which joined the two rooms. She waited for a minute or two with the knife gripped tightly in her hand and listened. Still she heard nothing. Slowly she opened the door and looked round. The hallway was empty but the carpet was now sprayed with blood across one side and there was a large patch of blood on the wall opposite the door. On the other side, clear of the blood and beside the door to the lounge, was a computer and a neat pile of files with a flash-drive on the top. Somebody had scrawled "For Sue and Dawn" on the top file. The front door appeared to be locked and there was no sign of John.

She double-checked that the door was secure and rushed back to the kitchen. As she arrived, Sue motioned for her to be quiet.

"There's somebody in the back yard," she whispered after a moment but although Dawn listened she could hear nothing.

"Where's John?" asked Sue, suddenly concerned for him.

Dawn shrugged her shoulders.

"He's gone. There's nobody there but the hall is covered in blood."

As the two women stared at each other trying to figure out what had just happened, they heard the squeal of brakes from the lane at the rear of the house and froze. Again they waited for ten minutes or more but there was no further sound or movement from anywhere around the house.

Eventually Dawn went through to the hall and picked up the files, the computer and the flash drive. As she returned to the lounge where Sue was returning with the twins, she opened the first file and glanced at the contents. She stopped dead in her tracks. The file had the Chancellor's name on it and the details on the first page and the contents made the hair on the back of her head tingle with shock.

She sat down on the sofa and looked at the names on the other files which included that of the Prime Minister. She took a sharp gasp of breath as she realised what she was holding.

Handing the flash-drive to Sue she said, "Have a look at this on your lap-top while I look through the rest of these."

Sue settled the twins in their rockers and plugged the device into one of the USB sockets of her lap-top. When it allowed her to open it she looked at a number of folders on the screen and noticed the top and most recent one was titled "Dawn Harper/Geoffrey Stanning".

She opened it and found that it contained a number of documents which read like newspaper articles. Opening the first one which was entitled "Prime Minister's PPS fathers secret love-child" she started reading.

"You will not believe what I am reading here about some of the biggest names in the government," said Dawn in astonishment.

"Want a bet?" replied Sue. "Because it can't be anything compared to what I'm reading here I'm afraid. Difference is, this is all about you."

58313184R00187

Made in the USA
Charleston, SC
09 July 2016